GW00480763

Heads Will Cinnamon Roll

Copyright © 2023 by London Lovett

ISBN: 9798390418147

Imprint: Independently published

A Scottie RAMONE COZY MYSTERY

HEADS WILL
Cinnamon Roll

LONDON LOVETT

one

. . .

"Wake up, Neverland Hall is let at last." The irritatingly cheery voice pierced through my dream in which I was baking the world's largest sourdough, but when I took it out of the oven it was a block of cheese. I yanked the quilt over my head as bright, also irritating, sunlight poured into the room.

"If you're trying to get me to believe that I just woke up at Pemberley, and Mr. Darcy is waiting for me in the breakfast room, it's not working," I mumbled through the cover before snatching it off my face. Nana was standing over the bed with her hands placed firmly on her hips, a gesture that would have looked far sterner if not for the pink striped apron with the smiling cow face. "And, for your information, it's Nether-field, not Neverland."

Nana tilted her head. Her long gray braid fell to the side with it. "Are you sure?"

"Positive." I turned away from her.

"No, I think you're wrong."

"Not going to have that debate at this hour in the morning." I pulled my pillow over my head.

"Then who lives in Neverland if not Mr. Bingley?"

I lifted the pillow just high enough to speak out from under it. "Peter Pan."

"Oh, well, it doesn't matter because it's neither Netherfield nor Neverland. It's Gramby Estate. Movers dropped storage containers there yesterday." I was under a pillow and making it more than clear that I had no intention of getting out of bed, but that didn't stop Nana from going right on with her conversation.

"Nana, I just want to sleep a few more hours, a few more days, maybe a few years." A month earlier, I'd been getting the final fitting on my wedding dress, a simple yet ridiculously expensive confection of lace, silk and tiny glass beads. After a harrowing few days where Nana went missing after her neighbor's shocking murder, I searched frantically for my one true family member only to find her in an old childhood hiding place. My future husband-to-be hadn't been the least bit supportive during my time of need, which made me question our entire relationship. In a matter of forty-eight short hours, I broke off the wedding, quit my pastry chef job in a Michelin Star restaurant, purchased an abandoned bakery, sight unseen, and moved back to my hometown of Ripple Creek. Through my flurry of rash decisions I had to convince myself that I was not moving back solely because my childhood crush (crush is almost too gentle of a word for how I once felt about Dalton Braddock) had moved back too. He was engaged, after all, and I was no longer thirteen and allowing my volatile hormones to make decisions for me. Or was I?

The mattress on the rollaway bed moved down a few inches. "Up and at 'em, Button," Nana said with a little less cheer. She placed her hand on my shoulder. "You'll see. It'll all work out."

"That was a good line to use when I was twelve, and I spilled orange juice on my history report." I tossed the pillow aside. She was using her secret smile, the one that she only used for me. It was a sly, little grin that deepened the lines on the right side of her mouth. Anyone else might have interpreted it as a smirk, but I knew what it meant— 'Scottie Ramone, it's you and me against the world, and the world doesn't have a chance'.

"This is no different than the orange juice disaster. And, as I recall, you still got an A, orange stain and all. You just need to get up, take a shower and start your feet moving toward opening a new bakery. And brush out that rat's nest on your head." She gave me a 'nice chat, now get up' pat on my hip and stood from the bed.

"I'm not ten years old. I'm a grown woman. If I want to wear a rat's nest on my head, I'll darn well wear one."

"You're a grown woman acting like a ten-year-old. By the way, I'm making waffles," she said as she reached the doorway.

"Waffles?"

"Yep."

"You should have led with that."

After a few moments contemplating my choices of staying in bed or getting up and eating homemade waffles, I realized there was no contest. Besides, I could always crawl back into bed with a belly filled with waffles.

I grumbled and growled like someone twice my age as I swung my legs over the sharp railing edge on the rollaway bed and put my feet on the wooden floor. I picked up my feet again, suddenly remembering how cold the bedroom floor could get, even in late summer. I pulled my feet onto the bed and hugged my knees to my chest. Outside the window, the painting-worthy landscape that grew thickly and with wild abandon around Ripple Creek and Nana's humble cottage, was alive with birds. The pastel blue branch of the spruce tree reverberated after a blue jay shrieked lightly, like a hawk, and took off.

Now that I knew what to expect, I placed my feet firmly on the floor. The floorboards still creaked in the same places as I padded across to the dresser. It was the only piece of orig-inal furniture from my childhood bedroom. Nana had kept the room exactly the same, with my boy band posters and my stuffed animal collection, well into my college years. I'd finally convinced her to turn it into her much needed art studio after I'd gotten a job and an apartment in the city. We'd had to push her easels and paint tables to the far side of the room to fit in the rolling bed. My own twin bed with the shiny white headboard was long gone. Our neighbor, Hannah Redmond, just happened to have the rolling bed in her sewing room. She complained 'it took up too much space anyhow'.

I'd worn my favorite oversized t-shirt to bed and decided it would do for a waffle breakfast. If I was going to act like a ten-year-old, I might as well go all the way. Wearing a time-softened, stretched-out t-shirt to bed was one of the freedoms I'd regained after leaving John. He had practically ordered me never to wear an oversized t-shirt to bed because it was tacky. The first time he said it, I pulled the pillows off the bed and slept on the couch… in the t-shirt. It was one of those hard, tufted modern couches that cost a ridiculous amount of money and was not comfortable to sit on, let alone sleep on. There it was—one of the many memories I needed to remind myself that I'd made the right decision not to marry Jonathan Rathbone. Rathbone. Another good reason. I didn't like the name. After a lot of arguments where I insisted I'd keep my own name, Ramone, because it was easier (and because his last name was better suited for a cartoon dog) John put down his proverbial foot and said he insisted I take his name. He put that foot down a lot. Slowly but surely, it was stomping away my own existence. Each time he tossed out a new command, he erased Scottie Ramone a little more.

My feet had gotten used to the cold floorboards. When I was a kid, I never wore shoes in summer. It was a tradition I'd decided to start again—except maybe outside. I still couldn't believe I'd wandered around on dry pine needles and gravel roads without shoes back then. I'd gotten soft in my old age.

I turned the sharp corner from my room into the bathroom. Nana's rat's nest description was fairly accurate. My shoulder length blonde hair stuck out in every direction, and there were a few good knots that let me know one round of conditioner was not going to do the trick. I smoothed my hands over it, but the clumps of tangles refused to be tamed. Then again, the rat's nest went rather well with my t-shirt. The collar had been so stretched it hung like a cowl necked sweater, and there were a few stains that looked as if I'd gotten a little careless with some hot cocoa at some point in time.

I heard Nana talking as my bare feet tapped the pine flooring in the narrow hallway. She was either talking to herself, something she did more than she cared to admit, or Hannah's cat, Mickey, had joined us for breakfast. The cat usually only showed up when bacon or sausages were cooking. I picked up my pace at the thought of crisp bacon topping off the waffles.

"Nana, I want extra butter on my waffle," I said before stopping cold in the doorway of the kitchen. Dalton Braddock, my childhood crush and Ripple Creek's new ranger, was sitting behind a double stack of Nana's buttermilk waffles.

"Morning, sunshine," he said as a wry reminder that this was not the first time I'd stumbled into the kitchen looking like something a cat might spit up only to find Dalton Braddock (again, and I cannot emphasize it enough, my childhood crush) sitting at our tiny, wobbly kitchen table.

"How is this happening again?" I muttered and made another fruitless attempt at smoothing my hair. Not that it would have mattered because Dalton had already seen the rat's nest.

I had two choices, other than melting into the floorboards and disappearing forever. I could turn and race back to my childhood bedroom slash painting studio, slam shut the door and pretend the last five seconds never happened. I could climb back in bed and stay there well into the future, at least long enough for Dalton to forget. That would, no doubt, be a long time. It would also mean missing Nana's buttermilk waffles. My other option was to stroll casually into the kitchen as if I'd meant to look exactly like this, and the fact that we had company, and rather significant company at that, meant nothing to me because, again, this was the way I'd meant to look. Since the latter meant buttermilk waffles, I willed my bare feet forward, tugging lightly on the hem of my t-shirt, which I now realized only covered about two inches of my thighs.

Dalton was smiling into his maple syrup drenched waffles. "Forgot what great legs you have," he said quietly so that Nana couldn't hear.

I sank down lower in my chair and avoided eye contact with him. The flowered wallpaper on the walls was starting to peel at the top. Outside the window, two robins were having a hot tub party in Nana's birdbath. Those were just two of the meaningless observations I made while trying to look everywhere but across the table.

I sighed with relief when Nana put a plate of waffles in front of me, extra butter. No bacon. The cat visit had been a false alarm. It turned out Nana was talking to Dalton and not

Mickey.

"When are you going to get that bakery going?" Dalton asked as he picked up his coffee.

Nana joined us at the table with her own plate. "She's going to get it going this week. Isn't that right, Scottie?" She said it so confidently, I almost believed it myself.

I sat up a little straighter. A sloppy slump wasn't helping. The humiliation was far from over, and I was more than keenly aware of just how terrible I looked thanks to my reflection in the coffeepot Nana placed on the table. I realized, then, that it was much easier to pull off teased, tangled and, if I was being honest, dirty, hair and a stretched out t-shirt when you were fifteen and not forty-one.

"I'm not so sure I'll be opening the bakery," I said curtly and filled my mouth with waffle to delay the follow-up. Since both of them were staring at me, with mouths slightly agape, I was certain there would have to be a follow-up. I chewed slowly, swallowed and took a long, dramatic sip of my coffee. My audience was still waiting.

I shrugged. "I'm thinking of just letting that family of raccoons have the place. They looked pretty comfortable when I opened the door and found them in various states of repose on the work table. I hate to evict them at a time when rents are high."

Nana rolled her eyes. "You'll have to excuse her, Dalton. She's been living on a diet of nacho flavored chips and cola for the last week, and she's not thinking straight."

"Thank you, *Evie*. Any other ways you can find to add to my total and utter embarrassment this morning?"

Dalton chuckled. "I forgot how entertaining it was to sit down to a meal with Evie and Scottie."

"Seems like you forgot a lot of things," I said with a half scowl.

"Ouch," Dalton said. "That might be my cue to finish. I'll let you get to your nacho chips and cola. Evie, the waffles were as good as I remembered." He smiled at me. "See, I didn't forget everything." He stood up. "Oh wait, I almost forgot—" he laughed to himself as he reached into the pocket of his olive colored work pants. "Here's the business card of a guy I know. He's a great general contractor. He could turn the raccoon hotel into that bakery you've always dreamed of." He slid the card across to me. "Thanks again for breakfast."

I waited for the screen door to snap shut and his truck to start up. "Nana, would it have killed you to let me know Dalton was sitting at the table? That's twice. I feel like I'm living in one of those terrible Ground Hog Day style loops, and every time I walk into the kitchen, my appearance gets a little more decrepit and Dalton gets a little more handsome."

Nana smiled over her cup of coffee. "He really is a picture, isn't he? That black hair and those dreamy dark eyes. And those broad shoulders."

I stared back at her as she listed his attributes, attributes that I had catalogued so well in my brain it was as if I'd created the man with my mind.

I focused back on my waffle. The morning wasn't a complete catastrophe. The waffles were crisp on the outside and buttery insides melted in my mouth.

"Maybe I could hang a necktie outside the kitchen on the

coat rack," Nana suggested. "That could be our signal. I understand a necktie means there's a visitor."

I chewed the waffle as I looked at her to see if she was serious. She was. "I think it means more than a visitor eating waffles," I said between bites.

"Are you sure? No, I think I'm right. It means there's a visitor."

"Yep, you're right. We'll go with your theory. How about you come into my room and—I don't know—try something like saying 'Dalton is here.' That'll probably be easiest, and that way you don't have to go out and buy a necktie."

Nana rocked her head side to side. "I suppose that works too."

two

. . .

S ince Nana made the waffles, I volunteered, reluctantly, to clean the kitchen. (Jeez, I really was regressing back to my teens.) A citrusy aroma filled the air as Nana poured herself a cup of tea and sat at the table. It had been so nice spending time with Nana, but it also made me feel as if I'd come full circle back to my starting point. I was living with my grandma again, and I had no job, no husband, or boyfriend, for that matter, and I was counting on things like homemade waffles to bring me joy.

"Hmm, this new honey orange tea is delicious. You should try some. Also, you were pretty rude to Dalton."

Nana was expert at working small irksome comments and pieces of advice into an otherwise everyday conversation.

I spun around with the measuring cup and drying towel in my hand. "I wasn't feeling too convivial because of this and this." I pointed to my hair and t-shirt.

"It's not Dalton's fault that you've let yourself go."

I placed the cup into the cupboard next to the large collection of measuring cups and spoons Nana had accumulated over the years. I shut the cupboard and leaned against the counter with the drying towel over my shoulder. "I have not let myself go. I've just decided to take a short, well-deserved break from everything societal, which includes brushing my hair and putting on makeup. Although, I'm really regretting not at least splashing on a layer of mascara before walking out to the kitchen."

Nana made a scoffing sound. I spun back around defensively. She blew on her tea before taking a sip. "Pour yourself a tea, Button. It'll relax you."

I was even back to being referred to as Button, my childhood nickname. I never minded it back then… if I thought about it, I didn't mind it now. It made me feel like grabbing my favorite stuffed teddy bear to curl up on the couch and watch cartoons. If only I could go back to those glorious days where missing Saturday morning cartoons was the worst of my troubles. I took her suggestion and poured myself a cup of tea.

Nana watched as I sat and took my first sip. "That citrus aroma wakes you right up, doesn't it? Makes you want to march right out that door and start a new business."

"Nice try. But the tea is good. What were you saying about movers dropping stuff off at the Gramby Estate?" I took another sip. "Gosh, I haven't seen that place in ages. Is it still spooky looking? My friends and I used to ride our bikes up there and try and scare ourselves. Worked pretty well a few times, too. Then we'd pedal away screaming in terror as if someone was chasing us. I can't believe someone bought it."

"The whole thing is a mystery." Nana took another sip of tea. "Even nosy posy extraordinaire, Charlene, from over on Oak Street, didn't have a clue, and nothing ever gets past that woman." Nana spoke as if she, too, wasn't usually privy to absolutely everything that happened in Ripple Creek. Many of the locals considered her some sort of wise old sage who always provided the best advice. Everyone came to her with their problems. I used to joke with her that she should set up one of those booths like Lucy in the Peanuts cartoons. If I thought about it, Nana was always behind most of my good decisions. Interestingly, she was very much not behind my decision to marry Jonathan. She was right about that near calamity. If I'd gone through with it all, I would have been living the life of Mrs. Jonathan Rathbone. Scottie Ramone would have been tucked away in a closet with a stack of useless wedding gifts.

Nana got up and poured herself a second cup of tea. My grandmother could have drunk the Queen of England under the table when it came to consuming tea.

"I guess as a kid I never really asked the story behind that house. For me, it was just a fun place to ride bikes for a good scare. Especially on Halloween."

Nana sat back down. "It was built in the late nineteenth century by Arthur Gramby. He was a very successful copper miner. He spared no expense on that place. For years, the town tried to buy the place from the family to refurbish it and use as a tourist attraction, but it was stuck in some kind of never-ending probate dispute. Last I heard, Arthur's great-great-granddaughter inherited it. Never heard about anyone coming to look at the house. From what I remember, Arthur's young wife died early in their marriage leaving him with three small children. He sent them off to live with relatives and concentrated on building himself a grand estate."

"That's right. Those three statues on the property are all of the same man, Arthur Gramby. Sharon Moore and I used to take turns climbing up behind him on the stone horse and yelling out 'Tally Ho!'"

"He must have been quite a vain man to have so many likenesses made. I understand the house was filled with his portraits as well." She took a sip of tea, and her secret smile appeared again.

"Uh oh, here it comes, my life changing lecture for the day. 'Scottie, there's nothing you can't do if you put your mind to it'," I said in a fair imitation of Nana's voice.

"No lecture, just a suggestion," she said with a dramatic pause for a sip of tea. "I'll have to get some more of this honey orange. It's perfect for summer. Which brings me to my suggestion—"

"Long segue, but go ahead. I'm listening but not guaranteeing anything."

"Tomorrow is the farmer's market on Town Road. Why don't you take that rolling cart I always used to sell my paintings at the market and fill it with something delicious from your baking repertoire. Nothing fancy. Something that everyone likes. Cinnamon rolls," she said enthusiastically.

"People would get a taste of how good your baking is, and you could let them know that the bakery is coming soon."

I hated to admit that it was a good idea. As usual, Nana was the wise old sage tossing out good advice. But did I have it in me?

"I don't know, Nana. I'd have to make some samples. I haven't baked cinnamon rolls in a long time."

Nana raised her hand as if in grade school. "Me, me, pick me. I want to be a taste tester for your samples. I'm sure Hannah would volunteer as well."

I cradled the teacup in my hands and turned it gently around between my palms. Part of me wanted to go full throttle with the idea, but there was still that part of me that said you deserve this break from the world. Go back to bed and wait for your favorite soap opera to start. Nana waited eagerly for me to give the whole plan a nod.

"I think I'll take a walk first, Nana. I really need to clear all these cobwebs out of my rat's nest."

Nana clapped once. "Good idea. Fresh air and a brisk jaunt will get all those body and brain parts moving."

"No promises," I said as I took my cup to the sink.

"Remember, the only important promises—are the ones you make to yourself," I said the last part along with Nana. It was one of her many sayings that I had ingrained in my head forever. My only worry was—I'd made these last big decisions so fast, I never had time to make that promise. How could I keep a promise that I'd never actually made?

three

· · ·

It was late summer, and it almost seemed as if all the warm air from the season had nestled in between the various peaks of the mountain range for good. I knew that was only wishful thinking. The comforting heat of summer would soon disappear, and a chill would fall over Ripple Creek from mid-fall until the middle of spring. The landscape in the Rockies was rugged and thick with pines and spruces. When the wind swept through just right it carried with it the energetic, spicy scent of the surrounding evergreens. This morning, the breeze was too gentle to fill the valley where Ripple Creek sat with that familiar Christmas-y aroma. But the air over our town was always crisp and refreshing, like a glass of water for a dry throat.

Chipmunks dashed around the forest floor litter as I tromped my way along the shortcut to Gramby Bridge. Not only had Arthur Gramby built himself a giant estate complete with mansion and coach house, he'd built a bridge to connect his estate to the half of town on the other side of Ripple Creek.

Ripple Creek had been categorized as a creek, but in the middle of spring, when the peaks finally decided to release their snowy caps, the creek became a river, swelling big and deep enough to hide the myriad of rocks and broken tree trunks. With a steady stream of melting snow and ice, the creek stayed full through summer. Rafting down it was a favorite pastime for those of us who grew up in town. It was also such a big lure for tourists, the local sporting goods store devoted an entire section to inner tube rentals.

My feet thumped the wooden planks on the bridge. It was an old but sturdy bridge that had been repaired ten years back after the creek had overflowed. As a kid, I rode back and forth across the old bridge without thought. As an adult, I was thankful for the earlier flood because the bridge was stronger with new fittings.

Once across the well traveled Gramby Bridge, a person could go east and land on Town Road and eventually the main part of town where shops lined both sides of the street. Traveling west off the bridge brought you to a road that eventually morphed into a dirt trail. Decades ago, when the estate was in its glory days, a layer of gravel led you up to the site. Most of that gravel had been washed away by weather and time. Back in the day, the path was wide enough for a large horse-drawn carriage. Now, it was barely wide enough for two people to walk side by side because nature had pushed itself in to reclaim its territory. I walked a good fifty yards until I noticed that the weeds and growth about two feet out from each side of the path had been flattened by large tires.

I reached the clearing that brought the entire estate into view. The three-story gray stone house sat stoically and confidently on its grassy knoll. The slate roof didn't look much worse for wear. Like Nana had said, Gramby didn't spare any expense when it came to his precious home. The rest of the house, however, looked as expected, like an abandoned building that had had more than its share of young, curious trespassers. Vines and weeds choked off the multi-step walkway up to the front door. The same untamed growth was making its way up the rough stone façade. It actually added some charm to the otherwise austere looking building. Long, vertical windows punctuated the sides of the mansion in groups of three. The wood trim had, at one point, been painted a grayish-blue, but only spots of the original color remained. Three tall chimneys jutted up high above the sharply steep roof. Each section of the home, four in all, had its own roof, making it look more like a collection of buildings rather than one family home.

Years ago, a portion of the fifteen-acre parcel had been a finely manicured garden (not easy in the Rockies) and the hillside itself had been carved into three distinct levels. Stone steps and a now parched stone fountain sat in the middle of the second layer. One could walk up the various sets of stone steps to get up to the top level of the garden where the house sat. There was no sign of the elegant garden anymore, just lush green grass that was slowly being overrun by whatever plants and trees had managed to get their seeds strewn there, whether by animal or wind or water. In a place like Ripple Creek, you had to work hard against nature to keep it tame. Nana always thought it a waste since nature had way more to offer than a neatly potted plant or seed packet.

With so much growth, it was much harder to traverse the site, even harder than when I was a kid riding through it on a bicycle. The stone steps to the top were loose and moss covered, but they'd held their positions in the hillside. I was breathing embarrassingly hard by the time I reached the top. I was still getting used to living at higher elevation. At least, that was the excuse I was going with.

Arthur Gramby's stern glower stared down at me at the top of the steps. The masterfully carved stone face had not weathered well either. Half of the thick, square shaped face was covered in green moss while the other had been pock-marked by the wind and heavy winter weather. The horse riding statue, where Arthur sat primly atop his steed, his fat belly protruding just a little over the saddle and the exact same glower (something told me it was a permanent expression) was positioned to the left of the garden. The shelter of the surrounding evergreens had spared it some of the damage that the first statue bore. A third statue, one where Gramby stood with his hands in his waistcoat pockets, was on the opposite side of the property.

The bright orange moving pods looked entirely out of

place. Nana was right. It seemed someone had plans to move into the Gramby mansion. Naturally, curiosity got the best of me. I wandered closer to the house to peer through a window. If some furnishings had been moved inside, it might give me a clue about who was moving in.

The first few windows were so covered in dirt, I couldn't see more than shadows in the rooms they were attached to. Even with the poor visibility, it seemed very little furniture had been moved inside. That made sense. I knew from experience the moving pods could be rented for several months, giving time for the new owners to do repairs, paint and clean before cluttering the rooms up with furniture and appliances. The two pods didn't look like they held nearly enough furniture to fill such a spacious house. Maybe this was only the first load.

I traipsed through some long tangles of bindweed. Small coppers fluttered over the weed's white and pink trumpet shaped flowers. I walked to a side of the façade that was mostly protected from the elements, like snow blowing from the north. One of the bottom windows was nearly free of layers of dirt. I smeared a little hole in the fine dust covering the glass pane and peered in through my self-made peephole. It gave me a view of the kitchen. An old black cast iron stove sat in one corner of the vast space. A table and two chairs, both leaning badly on broken legs, took up a good amount of floor opposite the stove. A large sideboard and hutch, obviously original to the kitchen, spanned half of the long wall. A few broken pieces of pottery sat in disarray on the shelves.

My eyes swept across and noticed something that stood out from all the antique and decaying pieces of furniture. It was a box of Frosted Flakes.

"See something that interests you?" a deep voice drawled from behind.

four

. . .

I t took me a second to realize that I hadn't imagined the
voice. I gasped and stepped back so quickly, I tripped
over the toes of his shoes. His long arms shot out. He caught
me before I landed on my backside.

"Gotcha." He helped me back to my feet, after which, all
manner of silliness flowed from my mouth.

"I promise I wasn't trying to break in, and I wasn't trespassing. Well, yes, I was kind of trespassing. But I used to
ride my bike up here as a kid, and it was always kind of this
iconic—you know—haunted house in the neighborhood. Not
that it's haunted. You definitely did not buy a haunted house.
I'm sure it's perfectly pleasant inside, and with your furniture, it'll be very cozy."

The man I'd babbled to like some kind of escapee from
the asylum was just under six-foot with a nice, muscular
build and light hazel eyes that seemed to be assessing just

how crazy I was. He ran his fingers through his dark brown, wavy hair. It hung almost to his shoulders and looked absolutely right on him. My age meter told me he was around forty.

He offered me his hand to free myself from the nightmarish tangle of bindweed that now seemed to be creeping over my shoes as if ready to grab on and hold me captive.

"The place is a dark, dusty dungeon, but unfortunately, I'm stuck with it." His smooth, deep voice went nicely with the rest of him. The pale green shirt he was wearing nearly glowed against his suntanned arms. We stopped on a clear spot of lawn. He once again offered me his hand. "Cade Rafferty, author of gothic thrillers and newest Ripple Creek resident. That is unless someone moved to town this morning, then I'm officially the town's second newest resident."

I shook his hand. "Scottie Ramone. Pastry chef and owner of a very abandoned old bakery on Town Road. I grew up in Ripple Creek and just recently moved back to do a restart on my entire existence."

He laughed. Some of the nervous embarrassment (which was probably quite evident on my face) subsided. "Now, that feat I have not tried yet, though maybe it's not a bad idea."

"Cade Rafferty," I repeated. It was a trick I used to remember people's names. "I thought you might be a Gramby."

"I am. Well, through my mother's side of the family. She inherited this place about twenty years ago and left it to me in her will."

"Oh, I'm sorry."

"That's all right. We hadn't spoken much since I gave up medical school to become an author."

"That's exciting. I mean, not the part about you not talking to your mother. That's always a sad thing. I lost my parents when I was seven, and my grandmother raised me here in Ripple Creek."

"Both parents. That must have been hard."

"It was but I was young enough that most of the memories are faded. You write books? Gothic thrillers? Not sure if I've ever read any of those."

"Count yourself within the majority then because it's a genre with a rather limited fan base. But I do all right." He gazed up at the three-story façade. Up close, the house was impossibly tall. "I was going to sell the place, then I looked up a photo and decided it was the perfect place to write gothic novels. I just wish it had a turret. I guess old Arthur didn't want it to look gaudy."

"I think he spent the money on statues of himself instead." I covered my mouth. "I'm sorry. I keep stepping in it. I don't mean to disparage your ancestor." I looked over at the one where Arthur was sitting astride his horse and thought about how often I'd sat behind him slapping the horse's rear and telling Arthur to giddy up.

"No apologies for my ancestor either. I heard he was a miserable man with few friends. There are at least half a dozen painted portraits in the house. Arthur Gramby was quite obsessed with his own likeness. I've never found people like that admirable or, for that matter, likable."

We strolled around the house. Two French doors led out

to a stone patio off the back of the house. A patio table and two chairs were set up on the pavers. A cup of iced tea sat next to a laptop and a paper pad with a great deal of hand-written notes.

"Would you like some iced tea?" he asked.

"No, I don't want to intrude."

His smile was just the right mix of cockiness and charm.

"Right," I said glancing down to hide the blush. "Guess it's too late for that since I've clearly intruded."

"Not at all. Feel free to walk these grounds anytime you like. There's a ridiculous amount of land around this old relic. As far as I'm concerned, no one should own this much of the earth." He motioned for me to sit at the table. I reluctantly pulled out a chair. It had been the first time I'd spoken to an interesting and, admittedly, handsome man in a long time. Some of the teenage self-consciousness that should have left me long ago but, unfortunately, had stuck around to torment me in times like this caused me to fuss with my hair. My blonde hair was thinner and straighter than I would have liked, and the dry mountain air always accentuated those two less than desirable attributes. Cade's thick and wavy hair, on the other hand, only seemed to be enhanced by the arid climate. It was smooth and shiny and, I was sure, soft, if one ran their hands through it. Not that I was imagining that scenario, of course. In fact, after the relationship fiasco I'd just been through, I'd resolved to leave men and marriage off my bucket list.

"You own a bakery?" he asked as he poured himself another glass of tea.

"I do. Only at the moment, it's occupied by a very unruly family of raccoons."

His laugh was the kind you wanted to hear over and over again. "I hate it when that happens. Especially the unruly ones." He sipped some tea. "I feel very impolite drinking this tea in front of you. Are you sure?"

"Yes, I just had breakfast. I'm fine."

"It's a shame about the raccoons. I, for one, am really fond of a good baked treat. Actually, now that I hear that out loud forget the *for one* part. I'm sure everyone in town is fond of a good baked treat." He leaned back in his chair and squinted one eye at me. "Are you talented?"

Another blush. There was nothing I hated more than talking about myself. I was sure it was because for five years I'd had to endure Jonathan's constant bragging about his own successes.

"Ah, you're one of those people who doesn't like to sing their own praises," Cade said. "An admirable quality. I guess I'll have to judge for myself someday. Hopefully, sooner rather than later."

"Do you like cinnamon rolls?" I blurted.

"Hmm, let me think. Yeast dough, sugar, cinnamon and lots of butter? Yes, I think those things fall into my stuff I like category."

"I guess that was a silly question."

"Not really. You'll have to excuse my sarcasm. It's a family curse. I can't seem to turn it off, even when I most want to." He sat forward. The sunlight made his hazel eyes look green. It seemed he had an enviable amount of long, black lashes to go with his thick head of hair. "Especially now when I'm trying not to scare off a new possible friend?" He said it as a question.

"I think we can work that out. I'm sort of new to town too, if you don't count the fact that half the people in town know when I had the chicken pox and when I got my first training bra." I slapped my hand over my mouth. "Can't believe I let that little nugget loose."

Cade had a way of laughing at the right time so you didn't feel embarrassed. "How on earth?"

"Yes, it sounds strange, but it'll all be explained when you meet my grandmother. She has zero filters, which can be a good thing whenever I need to hear straight talk, but it can also be a bad thing, like when you're thirteen, wearing your first bra and everyone in town is asking how you're doing. My grandmother is sort of an icon here in Ripple Creek. At fifteen, she found herself alone and pregnant. At the time, this town was very, how should I put this, communal."

"I've heard it was a big, wild hippie commune. At least, that was what my very prim, proper mother said. That was why she planned to sell the house the second the probate battle ended. She said she wasn't going to live with a bunch of free love, art-creating socialists."

I winced. "Wow, I guess your estrangement was probably a long time coming. How did she raise—"

"A man who gave up being a doctor for writing genre fiction? I think if she'd been a little more pliable and less aristocratic, I probably would have gone through with medical school."

"I see. So you were rebelling."

"That and I really hate the sight of blood."

A laugh burst from my mouth. "That does sound like an obstacle for a doctor. It would be like me hating the smell of yeast. Which reminds me—I need to get to the market and buy some ingredients." I stood up. He politely stood as well. "There's a farmer's market every Tuesday on Town Road. I'll be there tomorrow with my cinnamon rolls. You can judge for yourself." As I'd crossed the bridge, I wasn't entirely convinced that I wanted to bake anything for the farmer's market, but now, it seemed like a good decision. The handsome author with a hankering for a tasty baked good might have helped push me over the fence.

"I'll be there. I haven't had a good cinnamon roll in years."

I smiled at him. "Then prepare to be *rolled* over. See what I did there?"

"I did and very clever. See you tomorrow, Scottie. Trespass anytime."

I left with another blush and a new spark of anxiety. I was going to have to make some spectacular cinnamon rolls.

five

. . .

I typed out a list on my phone of all the ingredients I'd
need to make spectacular cinnamon rolls. The pressure
was on and not just because I bragged to Cade that he'd be
rolled over by my baked goods. I'd replayed that silly
moment in my mind several times until I forced myself to
stop overanalyzing, something I was prone to do when
feeling stressed. These cinnamon rolls would be my first shot
at gathering future customers for my bakery. I had no idea
why my confidence about my baking talents was at an all-
time low. If nothing else, that one aspect of life normally had
me brimming with certainty. I was blaming it on the hurri-
cane of emotions I'd been feeling in the last month. My life
was always on a straight forward trajectory, but I'd taken a
drastic U-turn. I needed to turn toward my future.

I was in luck. The morning tourist buses and shuttles had
already been through. They'd probably cleared Roxi's store of

all the homemade sandwiches and salads, but that was all right. I was there for flour, butter and cinnamon. Nana was sure to have all those ingredients in her kitchen. She enjoyed baking. But I didn't want to use up her supplies, and I planned on making a number of batches to achieve cinnamon roll perfection.

Roxi Tuttle had moved to town fifteen years ago. At that time, she was a thirty-something, newly divorced woman with a lump of money from her divorce settlement. Roger Pickering, the owner of the General Store, was looking to retire, so Roxi bought the place. She started making fresh sandwiches and salads for the tourists about ten years ago. They were such a hit, the tourist buses always made a point of stopping in Ripple Creek so people could grab their fresh sandwiches. Her wonderful sandwiches helped revive a town that had been fading into artsy obscurity. Roxi was a straight talker like Nana, and they became instant friends.

Roxi was putting new bags of chips on a much depleted spinning rack when I walked into the store. She was wearing her signature jeans and white t-shirt with a store logo which featured a moose standing with a sandwich in its mouth. The same sandwich eating moose smiled down at customers from the big sign over the front doors.

"Scottie, good to see you." Roxi shoved a bag of barbecue chips haphazardly on the stand and hurried over to hug me. She leaned to look past me. "Is Evie with you?" My grandmother and I had been such an inseparable pair while I was growing up, everyone always expected Nana to be with me.

"Just me. I need some ingredients. I've decided to sell cinnamon rolls at the street market tomorrow."

Roxi threw her arms halfway up and clapped. "I'm so glad to hear it. All of us are very anxious for you to open up that bakery. I can just smell the goodness now." She closed her eyes and took a deep whiff of the air to show me how committed she was to her bakery smell daydream. "I suppose you're going to need lots of butter. I just got a delivery from the dairy. How many pounds do you need?"

I scrunched up my face. "Can I get four pounds? I hate to deplete you of your stock."

Roxi waved off the concern. "Nonsense, the dairy delivers three times a week. I'll just add it back to the next order. Are you sure you only need four?"

I was going to need to wow people with these cinnamon rolls or my bakery dream might be over before it began. And butter was always a wow factor. "Actually, if you can make it five, that'd be great."

Roxi walked to the storeroom. I grabbed a cart and filled it with ten pounds of flour, two pounds of pecans, a three pound bag of powdered sugar, a bottle of vanilla, the good stuff, not the artificial one, a half-gallon of fresh cream and three bottles of cinnamon. I considered a bag of raisins. They would go with the vintage theme I was planning for the bakery, but I needed to keep it simple for now. The bakery had been closed for a long time. People were probably dying for freshly baked cinnamon rolls.

Roxi had returned with the boxes of butter by the time I reached the checkout counter.

I piled everything on the counter, and she rang me up. "Did you hear? Someone is moving into the Gramby Estate. There's been all kinds of wild speculation, like a reclusive, eccentric billionaire with his forty parakeets. Regina came up with that one." Roxi added an eye roll. Regina Sharpe owned the gift shop next door to the market. She was Roxi's main rival in the competition to be Nana's best friend. They were two very different women. Roxi was more serious and to the point, whereas, Regina tended to prattle on about things. I was pretty sure Nana preferred Roxi's company, even though Regina was much closer in age. But my diplomatic grandmother never let on that she liked one better than the other.

"An eccentric billionaire with a parakeet obsession. You know, someone like that would probably fit right in here in Ripple Creek, but I'm afraid Regina is wrong."

"Wrong about what?" Regina asked as she reached the counter. Her hair had gotten even whiter since the last time we spoke. "Scottie! You're out of bed. Evie mentioned you were having a little trouble adjusting. Don't get me started about adjusting." A statement that unequivocally meant she was going to get started about it. "After my Carlton died, I laid in bed for days staring at the ceiling wondering how on earth I'd get on with my life. So, one day—"

Roxi cut in. We'd both heard the story more than we cared to remember. "Scottie was just about to tell me about the people moving into the Gramby Estate. Weren't you, Scottie?" Roxi asked with a pleading eyebrow dance.

"I was. It turns out one of Arthur Gramby's descendants now owns the house. His name is Cade Rafferty."

Roxi stood taller behind her counter. "Wavy dark hair and hazel eyes that could render a woman speechless?" she asked excitedly. She gave herself a little shake. "Those weren't my words. Cindy and Louisa were making him a custom sandwich. He didn't want mayonnaise, and for some reason, that particular sandwich required two sandwich makers." She rolled her eyes again. "They happened to mention his eyes." Roxi seemed sorry she'd given him such a glowing review.

"Well, Cindy and Louisa were right," I said to make her feel more comfortable. Otherwise, I knew, too well, Regina would be giving her a hard time about it later. "He's very handsome, and he's a writer. We spoke for a few minutes this morning when I—when I happened to see him on my walk."

"This is exciting," Regina said. "Two new people in town."

"Who else?" I asked.

"Didn't you see? It's right next to your bakery," Regina said. "The new bookstore, Nine Lives Bookshop, is opening in a week."

I chuckled. "A bookstore owner—it's probably some hunched over old man or lady who owns two cats and likes dusty old furniture to clutter the shop."

I was so busy stereotyping bookshop owners, I hadn't noticed Roxi's discreet hand motioning me to stop. She plastered on a big smile for someone behind me. "Morning, Esme."

I turned. The woman behind me looked to be in her late thirties. She was taller than average, maybe five foot ten and very thin with black hair cut short. Most importantly and horrifying of all, she was wearing a green canvas work apron with the words Nine Lives Bookshop embroidered across the front.

She stuck out her hand. "Hello, I'm Esme, the bookshop owner. I'm not quite hunched yet, but I do have three cats."

My face felt as hot as the sun. "I'm sorry. I was just gabbing with my friends. I do not think all bookstore owners are hunched over octogenarians with old dusty couches."

Esme laughed, which immediately made me think she was someone I could be friends with. "Actually, that's pretty accurate. I guess I'm an anomaly. Although, I do hope to one day aspire to that hunched over octogenarian status. You're Scottie."

"Yes, Scottie with the big, opinionated mouth. Nice to meet you."

Esme placed a package of chocolate chip cookies on the counter. "Nice to finally meet you. Can't wait for the bakery. I heard you were a Paris trained pastry chef." I was at a disadvantage. I hadn't heard anything about the bookstore owner. I'd been so selfishly mired in my own pity party, I hadn't even noticed that the bookstore was taking shape right next to my derelict bakery.

"Thanks. It's going to take some work. Roxi, add her cookies to my total." I paid Roxi and looked at the counter full of ingredients, including heavy bags of flour. "I just realized I walked here, Roxi. Can you put this stuff aside? I'll go home and get my car."

"Absolutely."

Esme picked up the cookies. "Thanks for these." We both waved to the 2Rs, as I usually referred to them, both mentally and whenever I needed a shortcut while talking to Nana about her two best friends.

"If you have a second," Esme said as we stepped outside into the bright late morning sun. "I've got some ideas for the outside of the bakery."

We both glanced across the street. Her bookshop had been painted with a rich lacquered forest green paint. Structurally, it was much more attractive than the brick monstrosity I'd slapped down good money for. The bookshop had four large windows with transoms on top of each. The front door was all glass as well, and there was a neat little transom with a bold patterned piece of stained glass. A long sign with the name Nine Lives Bookshop was painted in shiny gold and black. The building had been home to everything from a shoe repair shop to a stationery store. It had changed hands a lot. My building had an all brick façade. There were some nice front windows, but the glass needed to be replaced. Most of it was cracked or scratched. And that was it. There were no adornments or pretty transoms or stained glass. It looked particularly pathetic next to the bookshop.

I turned back to Esme. "I'll take any advice you have to give."

six

. . .

I had a lot of baking to do, but after seeing the outside of the bookshop, I decided not to pass up a chance to hear Esme's ideas for the dreary brick building where I hoped to start a bakery.

"Come on inside first, and I'll show you around the bookshop. You can meet Trina, Salem and Earl." She turned back to me as she opened the door. "I haven't gotten everything shelved yet, but you can get the general idea."

I stopped in the middle of the store, in the small space that wasn't lined with bookshelves or boxes of books waiting to find their place on the shelf, and looked around. Small reading nooks, complete with comfy looking chairs, had been set up in various places around the store. There were three tiny but uniquely different wooden tables surrounded with different colored wooden chairs.

"I'm hoping I get some of your bakery spillover," Esme

said as she put the cookies away. "I set out tables and chairs, so people can enjoy your goodies while they're reading or working on homework."

"What a terrific idea." Now, I was really feeling pressure to open up that darn bakery. I just needed to get my enthusiasm back for the project. I'd dreamt of opening my own vintage style bakery for years, ever since I realized working in an industrial sized kitchen for a high dollar restaurant wasn't making me happy. I'd let too much emotional clutter keep me from moving forward. I was sure Jonathan had moved right on with his life, hardly considering the end of our wedding anything more than a blip in his life's plans. I needed to do the same. Of course, it didn't help that his mom kept sending me bills from the cancelled wedding. I told John I'd pay his mother back all the money his parents spent on the event. Although, it wasn't terribly fair considering the extravagant wedding and reception had been her idea. It wasn't what I wanted at all. It was one of the reasons I wanted out of the whole thing. After giving my almost mother-in-law the reins, it slowly but surely became her wedding and not mine. Just like in our relationship, there wasn't even one speck of Scottie Ramone left by the time it was all done.

A soft body twirling around my ankles pulled my focus down to my feet. A smallish cat with a shiny black coat stared up at me with amber eyes. I leaned down to pet him.

"That's Salem. He's the flirt of the group." Esme walked over to one of the big chairs. A small white head with perfectly pointed ears and one blue and one green eye popped up when Esme gently tapped the arm of the chair.

"This is Trina, my little princess. She can't hear a thing, so she's a little more skittish. And, curled up on top of the books in that box"—she pointed to a tall box—"is Earl. He's that big ole uncle who belches after Thanksgiving dinner and then opens the top button of his pants after he plops on the couch. He's lovable, slovenly and doesn't give a hoot what people think."

"I never had an uncle. Both my parents were only children, but growing up here, we always invited George Freemont from down the road to Thanksgiving, and yes, I remember the belches and the top button release."

Esme had sapphire blue eyes that contrasted beautifully with her black hair. Her complexion was fair with a light spray of freckles across her nose and cheeks. Sorrow washed over her face. "I'm so sorry to hear about your parents. Roxi told me what happened."

It seemed Roxi had been doing a lot of gabbing and narrating. "I was very young. Growing up here and with my grandmother was all a kid could ask for. How about you? I've been sort of *indisposed* and haven't had much time to talk to Roxi or Regina or anyone else, for that matter. As you might have noticed with my ignorant comment earlier, I haven't heard anything about you."

"That's all right. Roxi mentioned that—"

I put up my hand. "I'm sure she's filled you in on everything because Roxi is thorough if nothing else. I've had a turmoil filled month, but I'm getting my sea legs back, or, in my case, my Pillsbury Doughboy legs."

Esme laughed. It caused the elusive box sleeper Earl to lift his head to make sure he wasn't missing anything.

"Oh my gosh, is that just one cat?" I asked and headed his direction. "His head is as big as a softball." I reached the box. Earl's plump, enormous body filled out the rest of the box as if he was liquid and not solid. I scratched him behind the ears, and he purred contentedly.

"He was a massive kitten too. I felt bad for his mom. I've seen him stare down dogs twice his size. They always cower in confusion because he's so much bigger than the usual cat. I got him from a shelter in Florida. That's where I grew up. My parents still live there."

"From Florida to the Rocky Mountains—that's a drastic change in climate."

"That's why I picked this place. Do you know how boring it is to wake up every day to warm sunshine?"

I patted Earl's head. "Must have been very difficult," I said with a dramatic shake of my head.

"I know, it sounds ridiculous when I say it out loud, but there are no seasons in Florida. I wanted seasons. I wanted crisp fall days with glowing colors in the trees, white winters with hot cocoa, lush springs with wildflowers and lots of animals. Trust me, alligators are not the kind of wildlife you stop and look at with awe or admiration. I've already seen more wildlife here in three months than I've seen my whole life in Florida."

"Well, you might be singing a different tune in the dead of winter, but I agree, the seasons are wonderful up here."

"Shall we go outside? I'll tell you my ideas for your

bakery." She stopped. "Gosh, I hope I'm not overstepping the line here. I really want the two of us to be good friends."

"You're not overstepping at all, and I'm sure we'll be great friends." And I meant it. It wasn't often I met someone who I instantly thought I could befriend. Esme definitely fit that bill.

"By the way," Esme said as we reached the front of my shop, "there seemed to be a family of raccoons going in and out a broken grate in the back of your building. I used cat food to lure them out, then I covered up the hole. I hope that's all right."

"Of course, and I owe you one. I wasn't sure how I was going to get those little stinkers out of my store."

"Great," she smiled. "Now you've got one less thing to worry about."

"Absolutely." It seemed the events of the morning only had one clear message—Scottie Ramone, it's time to get your act together.

seven

. . .

E sme had some brilliant ideas for the front of the bakery. She suggested I paint the dreary, worn bricks a creamy white, install some multi-paned windows and French doors, add a striped awning over the entire stretch of windows and have the name of the bakery scrawled out in a fancy script across the front of the building. I liked all of her ideas.

My footsteps were lighter as I reached the bridge. A vehicle rumbled and rattled behind me. I hated crossing the narrow bridge with a vehicle, so I stopped and waited for it to pass. The older, jalopy-ish van tilted side to side as it barreled toward me. I stepped farther off the road, into the dried weeds to keep out of its path. An older man, possibly in his fifties with meaty arms and a thick head of gray peppered hair, leaned out the driver's window. He didn't seem to notice that he'd all but driven me off the road with his ungainly van jumbling along at top speed. A loud whistle split the air and caused several birds to leave the trees above. He grinned at me and whistled again before finally focusing back on the narrow bridge ahead. The side of his van had large lettering, some of which was scratched off but not so much to make it illegible. Saul Fixes All. I'd heard of Saul the handyman before but never had a firsthand encounter. It wouldn't bother me too much if it was the last time we had an encounter. I watched as his van tires left the wooden bridge. The van creaked with old age as the tires hit the road. Dust kicked up behind the tires as Saul stepped on the gas again. It was easy to guess where he was heading because there was only one house on the gravel road to the west. It seemed my new friend, Cade, had hired himself a handyman.

I returned to the bridge. My phone buzzed with a text. There was nothing more deflating than seeing the name Margaret Rathbone come up on the screen. With great trepidation, I clicked on it. "Miss Ramone"—she'd switched to the formality after I ducked out on *her* wedding—"I've forwarded another bill to your email. It's for the ice sculptures. Please pay it promptly as the bill is in my name."

I blew a loud raspberry from between my lips. "Ice sculptures were your idea, *Mrs. Rathbone.* And they were a stupid idea too." I jammed the phone back into my pocket. I wondered when the trail of bills would end. I hadn't even heard about the ludicrous swan ice sculptures until a week before the wedding.

My light footsteps suddenly felt heavy, and my feet pounded the last few wooden planks on the bridge. The notion of baking many batches of cinnamon rolls, not an easy feat, sounded far less appealing than it did five minutes ago. Maybe I'd try for the next farmer's market. Nana's couch probably needed some company, and there was a new bag of chips in the cupboard.

I reached Rainbow Road, my head once again feeling heavy with sadness. Nana was sitting on the front porch reading a book. She looked up over the rim of her glasses. "Good walk?"

"It was great right up until a few minutes ago," I muttered. My feet remained heavy as I made my way to the cupboard and then to the couch. I plopped down as if my legs were no longer controlled by muscles. I ripped open the bag so fast chips flew everywhere. I was just picking them up as Nana stepped into the house.

"Oh dear. I was hoping the walk would have helped."

"It did but the fix was only temporary. I'm back to my evil ways." I held up the badly ripped chip bag. "I'm even opening chip bags like I'm some kind of desperate chip junkie. Everything was going along swimmingly, then my near-miss mother-in-law sent me another bill. This one was particularly egregious, three thousand dollars for ice swans."

Nana sat down primly next to me. "Scotlyn—" Her straight posture and the use of my given name meant she was about to deliver some tough love. "First of all, between your parents and your late paternal grandmother, you have a trust fund that would make that snooty Crystal Miramont green with envy. Pay the bill and then forget about it."

I groaned as I rolled down to rest my head against the arm

of the couch. "You know how I hate using that money. It was supposed to be for mom and dad, for their fun, for their vacations, for the future they never had." Thinking about the grand sum of money my parents left behind always brought back that same sadness I felt the day they died. Because my trust fund was connected to their tragic deaths, I was always reluctant to touch it. Since my dad had been an only child, my late Grandma Katherine's estate had been left to me. It was no small chunk of change. The Ramones had been in shipping and exports, and my father grew up very privileged. And while my Grandma Katherine had soft hands, always smelled like lavender and was fine as far as grandmothers went, I was forever grateful that my mom had had the forethought to make sure her mom, Grandma Evie, raised me if they both died.

"You're not that seven-year-old girl anymore. Pay those bills, get past that wedding, and be thrilled with the notion that you missed having that woman as your mother-in-law."

I sat up and slumped back against the couch. "Definitely dodged a bullet there."

Nana put her hand on my leg. "Button, you have too much to offer to spend your days on a couch eating potato chips." She paused and bunched her brows as she reached for something under her bottom. Her hand emerged with a pile of chip crumbs. "Honestly, Scottie," she said in her motherly tone, a tone she still used when I was acting childish. Without warning, she snatched the bag from my hands. More chips flew.

"Hey, I was eating those."

"No more. You're not a pouting teen anymore. You're a middle-aged woman, and that much sodium will give you high blood pressure."

I turned my face toward her without lifting my head from the back of the couch. "This has been a great pep talk. Is there anything else you'd like to add, like, I don't know—just think, Button, you're more than halfway to eighty and all you've got to show for your life is that there are chip crumbs all over the couch?"

"Well, hello there, Sorry Sally, haven't seen you in a few years," Nana taunted.

"Oh no you don't. No bringing back Sorry Sally." I sat up straighter deciding the slump wasn't helping my argument. "I'm not ten anymore. No Sorry Sally." Whenever I moped around the house as a kid, because my friends all had something to do or because summer vacation was coming to an end, Nana would call me Sorry Sally. She wouldn't stop until my mood lifted, which it usually did quickly because I hated to be called Sorry Sally.

Nana broke character this time. She laughed and patted my leg again. "That nickname used to get you so mad. But it worked."

"Can't argue with that."

"All kidding aside," Nana said, "I need you to get up, start your baking and be ready to knock the socks off people tomorrow at the street market. You need to get your independence back. Jonathan zapped you of all your inner strength. Besides that, I want my art studio back."

"Ah, I see. You just want me off your couch and out of the house."

"Yep," she said as she stood up. "Once you're used to an empty nest, having the fledglings come back as full grown adults, makes for a crowded nest." She headed toward the kitchen.

"So, you're going to throw me out on the street?" I asked.

She stopped in the kitchen doorway and twisted back. The lines on her face were getting deeper, but her eyes still sparkled with energy and youth. "I don't think it's possible to throw someone with a sizable fortune out on the street, Button. Now, go get the ingredients you need for cinnamon rolls. I'm looking forward to tasting them." She headed into the kitchen.

I sat forward. "The ingredients. Oops." I hopped up, newly energized, and grabbed my car keys. Nana's pep talks were mostly unorthodox, but darn, if they weren't effective.

eight

. . .

I returned with the ingredients I bought for cinnamon rolls. It was close to noon. That meant there wouldn't be enough time to trial and error my way to the world's best cinnamon roll. I would go with what I knew and trust my baking instincts, something I'd had more than one baking instructor tell me I had. The farmer's market, even at this late date in summer, was always crowded. I needed to make six dozen cinnamon rolls to get my product out there and, with any luck, generate some buzz.

I heard Nana muttering unseemly words as I stepped past the garage. I walked around to the side door and found my eighty plus grandmother standing on a less than sturdy step stool reaching up high for a cart.

"Nana, get down from there."

She realized her reach was not going to be enough. I held

out my hand, and she used it to step gingerly down from the stool. "I wanted to get the rolling cart down so I could give it a good wash before tomorrow." The old rolling cart was a metal cabinet set between four wheels. Nana had painted it with mountain scenery. It had been a long time since she wheeled her art to the market to sell her work. She'd slowed down a lot in her painting and only occasionally sold a piece of art.

"I'll get it down after I finish making my dough. I need to get it proofing."

Hannah met us at the door as we headed inside. "I understand there is a taste tester position to fill," she said cheerily. "Just point me in the direction of the cinnamon rolls."

"I'm afraid the cinnamon rolls are still just bunch of separate ingredients, Hannah. But if you come back in two hours, there should be some nice hot buns to sample."

Nana held out her hand for Hannah to take. "In the meantime, you can come inside for tea."

Hannah gladly accepted the offer. I carried in the rest of the groceries while Nana brewed some green tea. The business card Dalton gave me was sitting propped up against the toaster. It was Nana's not so subtle way of saying 'don't forget to call the contractor'. I put the card in my pocket. The bakery was definitely going to need a contractor. With the outside sorted, thanks to Esme, I needed to focus on the hard part, the interior. There were walls to move, a kitchen to create and I was sure there were plumbing and electrical issues to deal with. The derelict condition of the building's interior was one of the things that had caused me to hibernate in my bed. The realtor was beaming when he handed me the keys, as if he'd just made the proudest sell of his career. Once inside, I realized his ear to ear grin was more of a pity smile. The word *sucker* might have been going through his head as well.

I kneaded, stretched and folded my yeast dough into a nice smooth ball and set it in the oven to proof. Nana's tiny kitchen was going to be far from ideal for baking dozens of cinnamon rolls, but I used to bake cookies and pastries in my tiny Paris apartment for practice so I knew how to manage. Still, an expansive bakery with proofing ovens, large refrigerators and massive tables for rolling, shaping and kneading would be a dream. Thinking about it caused me to reach into my pocket and pull out my phone.

Cell phone reception in Nana's house was sketchy at best, so I left Nana and Hannah to their tea and their chat while I stepped out into the midday sunshine. The sun was always stronger and brighter up in the mountains. I wandered over to the shade of the pine in Nana's front yard. Two western tanagers, with their flame red heads and orange bellies, were enjoying the grape jelly Nana had left out for the sweet toothed birds in the neighborhood. They left their sticky treat reluctantly with my arrival.

Mike Stanford was the name on the card. He answered on three rings. "Mike here." I could hear hammering and clanging in the background and plenty of voices too. I worried my job might be too small for him.

"Hello, my name is Scottie Ramone. Dalton Braddock gave me your—"

"Dalton? How is he doing?"

"Uh, he's fine, I guess. He gave me your card. I have a building that needs to be transformed into a bakery. He thought you might be able to help."

"Sure, sure. Where are you located?"

"Ripple Creek."

"Hmm, that's a little farther out than I like to go, but I'll make an exception since you're a friend of Dalton's. I can come by Friday and give it a look. Let's say two?"

"That works. I'll text you the address."

"Perfect. Oh and say hello to Dalton."

"I sure will." I had no doubt I would run into him in Nana's kitchen again while looking my finest, I thought wryly.

I sent off the address and headed back inside. Aside from a fluffy, tender yeast roll, I needed a spectacular filling and glaze, something that would have people talking about my rolls. I also wanted to keep it a little vintage, something that inspired a fun wisp of nostalgia. Caramel rolls were always popular in the fifties and sixties.

Nana and Hannah looked up from their teas.

"What do you ladies think about a caramel rich filling, butter, brown sugar and chopped pecans? I'll top it with a brown sugar glaze, the kind that sticks to your fingers and, therefore, requires a great deal of licking. I'll make some simple, cinnamon-filled rolls with a regular glaze too for the traditionalists."

Hannah clapped. "I love it. My grandmother used to make caramel buns every Easter." She slumped a little. "Gosh, I miss her."

I nodded. "See, that's what I'm hoping to create. Caramel gooeyness that makes everyone wish they were a kid again, licking caramel, buttery goodness off their fingers."

"Well then, Button, it seems you've got your recipe. Now, let's get on with that taste testing."

nine

. . .

Days were still long enough that there was daylight left after dinner. Nana had made a delicious salad with some of her last garden cucumbers and tomatoes. We'd both eaten far too many of my sweet rolls. Fresh salad was the only thing that sounded good. I'd done some trial and error with the filling. In the end, a delicious, finger licking treat came together. Nana didn't have enough trays, so we had to create some out of flat boxes lined with parchment. Her small kitchen was filled from one end to the other with rolls all sitting in neat lines in their pools of glaze and caramel.

Nana had fallen asleep on the couch, her book upside down on her chest as she snored softly. I stepped outside for some fresh air. I'd been in the kitchen the entire afternoon. As deliciously as my rolls had turned out, I was officially saturated with the aroma of butter, brown sugar and cinnamon.

I sat on the front steps breathing in the fresh pine filled air when a horse's hooves clip clopped on the road. A small breath caught in my throat. For a moment in time, I was in a romance novel, and the handsome Duke of Ripple Creek was heading toward me on his tall horse. Dalton had pulled on a black cowboy hat to add to the look. (Shame he didn't have a black top hat. That would have been a picture.) It was only the second time I'd seen Dalton on Kentucky, a gentle but sturdy blue roan gelding. Dalton was wearing a dark blue t-shirt, jeans and cowboy boots, not his usual official attire. I rather liked this country version of Dalton, though the uniformed one wasn't bad either.

Those same butterflies that had circled my stomach when I was thirteen and about to talk to Dalton Braddock had returned. They hadn't slowed down with age. I strolled out to meet him. Kentucky immediately turned his head for me to rub his nose. I had to squint slightly as I stared up at him. "What brings you out here, Cowboy Braddock?"

Dalton tipped his hat. "Howdy, ma'am."

"Ew, no use of ma'am, cowboy slang or not."

"Duly noted." Dalton leaned forward and patted his horse's neck. "Kentucky was bored, and I had the afternoon off so we decided to go out for a ride. I was looking forward to doing patrols on horseback, but I rarely get the chance."

"That's nice you have the day off."

"Just the afternoon. I've got to drive up to the resort tonight. They've been having problems with vandalism. The culprits have been using the dark of night as their cover."

"That doesn't sound like a fun assignment. I'm sure Crystal appreciates having the local law enforcement on speed dial." I wasn't sure I should have said it. Unfortunately, that self-reflection didn't pop up until the words were already out of my mouth. He could have easily taken offense at what I said. Instead, he grew quiet. "I'm sorry, I didn't mean to imply that you're giving the resort special consideration over the rest of the mountainside."

His mouth tilted. "You were kind of implying that."

I nodded. "Maybe I was. But it makes sense. That's where all the rich people and high-end businesses are. They make much better targets than those of us down here in our tiny, ramshackle cabins."

"My cabin is not ramshackle. It's quaint," Nana called from inside.

I shook my head. "Thought she was sleeping. There were snores and everything. Speaking of Crystal, how are the wedding plans going?" The question pulled his mouth down in a frown. "Another bad topic," I said. "You'll have to forgive me. I haven't been too social lately."

Kentucky took a step closer to Nana's garden, hoping that we wouldn't notice a fifteen hundred pound horse casually stepping over to the cucumbers and tomatoes. Dalton tugged him back gently. "Not today, buddy. Remember what happened the last time you decided to eat a bunch of raw tomatoes." Kentucky released a soft, disappointed snort. "Crystal is planning a wedding fit for royalty. 'A girl only gets married once'," Dalton said in a high pitched tone.

"Definitely not true," I said.

"I know that, but she's not great at listening to anything

that isn't sitting in her own head. I wanted something simple."

"A meadow ceremony and a picnic for the guests with maybe a few folk singers strumming under a shade tree." It rolled out without hesitation because that was my idea of a dream wedding.

"Exactly," he blurted. "That's exactly what I consider to be the perfect wedding. We're already waiting an extra year because the band Crystal wanted was booked out for months. Last I heard, though I've been trying to ignore most of it to keep my sanity, she's planning on having bagpipes play as the guests arrive."

I shielded my eyes to get a clearer view of him sitting up so high. "Is Crystal Scottish?"

He shook his head. "Not even one single hair on her head. I'm probably more Scottish and only because I traveled there once with my parents and they made me put on a kilt for photos. That is my entire claim to my non-existent Scottish heritage."

"Bagpipes are cool," I suggested weakly.

"It's not just the bagpipes. It's everything. She's changed her mind about the reception dinner four times. Local caterers are no longer taking her calls, and she can't understand why." The wedding seemed to be causing some friction between them. I was trying to show sympathy, not the touch of glee I was actually feeling. "Oh well, enough about that. It only aggravates me to talk about. Onto something new." The saddle leather squeaked as Dalton sat up and took a deep breath. "Why does Evie's house smell like my grandmother's butterscotch blondies?"

"Aha, another nostalgic response courtesy of my sweet rolls. I made caramel and cinnamon rolls. I'll be selling them tomorrow at the farmer's market. Drop by if you have time."

"You're baking. Does that mean we can expect a new bakery and I can stop eating those stale pastries from the ranger station's vending machine?"

"I'm hoping that will be the case. I called your friend, Mike. He's coming by Friday. He asked about you."

"We went to high school together. We were pretty good pals before we went our separate ways. His company is based down at the bottom of the highway. Did you tell him where your bakery is located?"

"Yes, and he said he'd make an exception because I'm friends with Dalton Braddock."

Dalton couldn't hold back a smile. "I'll have to check in with him when he's up here. Glad I could help. It's my duty as an important member of the community to see that we get good pastries and breads."

Kentucky was getting antsy. He pawed at the ground a few times.

"You two better get on with your ride," I said.

"Yep," Dalton said in a cowboy drawl. He reached up with one hand and lifted the hat politely. "Later, m—" He rolled in his lips. "Nope, not going to make that mistake twice."

I laughed. "You're a fast learner. And while we're on the topic, lil' lady is not allowed either."

It was his turn to laugh. He lifted the reins. Kentucky snorted, ready to move along. The horse took a few steps, then Dalton stopped him. He looked back at me. "Hey, Scottie—"

I shielded my eyes from the sun. "Yeah?"

"I know you've been having a hard time getting used to all this change, but, for what it's worth, I'm really glad you moved back to Ripple Creek."

His words and the sincere tone that went with them caught me off guard. I'd been such an emotional wreck for a month, feeling very sorry for myself at the same time, my throat instantly tightened. It was hard to reply. "Thanks." It was all I could croak out.

They rode off into the proverbial sunset, cowboy and his faithful horse. I had a hard time pulling my gaze away. The screen door squeaked bringing me out of my movie like daydream.

"He sure drops by a lot," Nana said in a tone that could not be misconstrued.

"He's engaged to a beautiful, rich woman," I reminded her unnecessarily. It might have been more for me.

"I heard him out here complaining about the wedding plans. Crystal isn't right for him. He'll figure that out soon enough."

I looked at her and rolled my eyes. "You find me a man who can walk away from a blonde with a gorgeous figure and a large bank account, and I'll show you man who doesn't exist."

I headed back inside. Before the screen door shut, Nana

continued. "You have a large bank account. He just doesn't know it."

"He doesn't need to know it." I stopped and peered through the opening I'd left with the screen door. "And, minor point, I'm not gorgeous."

Nana made a pfft sound. "Gorgeous is overrated."

"If only that were true," I called to her as I headed into my room. It had been a long day, especially for someone who had hardly left her house or bed for a month. I needed a nap before bedtime.

ten

. . .

I t took a lot of coaxing, but I'd talked myself out of bed early to get ready for the street fair. I knew from helping Nana with her painting sales it was always best to get there before the start of the event. Otherwise, you were trying to get organized with customers already needing attention. I hoped to get a spot right in front of my shop, ugly as it was in its current state. It would give future customers a reference point when they came back to buy another one of my treats.

I was busy pushing napkins into a Ziploc bag when someone knocked urgently on the front door. Nana looked up from her cup of coffee with an expression of alarm. "Who on earth could that be at this hour?" She started to stand.

I put my hand up. "I'll go first."

The knocking grew more intense. My heart sped up thinking whoever was on the other side might have been chased up to our door by a bear or rampaging moose. I glanced cautiously through the small window at the top of the door and felt some degree of relief when I saw it was Hannah. However, the pale, scared look on her face reminded me of my bear theory. I yanked the door open prepared to go into my 'big and loud' act if a bear had followed her into the yard. But it was just Hannah. She half stumbled inside and clutched Nana's arm for support. Her breathing was fast and sharp, and aside from the red windburn on her cheeks, her skin was white.

"They've all had their heads cut off," she said between gulps of air. "Someone beheaded them."

Nana's hand flew to her chest. "My goodness gracious, who, Hannah? Who had their heads cut off?" Nana was losing some color too. I took both women by the elbows and led them over to the couch.

"Sit down before you pass out, Hannah," I said. "Then you can tell us what's happened." Her first words 'they've had their heads cut off' were so alarming, I would have preferred to fend off a bear.

Hannah sat down and pulled a handkerchief out of her pocket to wipe her forehead. "I rode here so fast, I thought my heart might burst." That did not seem like an exaggeration. She blotted her face.

Nana placed her hand on Hannah's leg. "Now tell us, dear. Whose head? What's happened?"

With the way Hannah had knocked and entered, one could almost believe that the whole town had been massacred by some axe wielding madman. Then Hannah looked at both our faces, now hovering with horrified curiosity, and she sank back slightly contrite. "Well, it wasn't a person, but it was still awful."

Nana's hand flew to her mouth. "Geese? Squirrels?"

Hannah smiled coyly and pushed her handkerchief in her pocket. "No, nothing like that. It was the statues up at the Gramby Estate. All of Arthur Gramby's various heads are lying in the weeds and grass, each statue chopped off cleanly at the neck." Hannah ran her finger across her neck to add a visual. It seemed she was revisiting her very dramatic entrance and feeling a little silly about the whole thing. She placed her hand on Nana's and forced a grin.

Nana looked back at her fully dismayed. "My gosh, Hannah, you stumbled in here looking as if you'd just discovered many headless bodies."

"Well, Evie, I have. It was a horrid sight. I rode my bicycle up to the Gramby Estate." She smiled and shrugged. All of the color had returned to her cheeks and then some. "I thought I might catch a glimpse of the new owner. I often ride that way instead of towards town on street market day. Too many trucks and cars on Town Road. I got off my bike and hiked up those old, crumbling steps. Twisted my ankle too."

"You deserved it." Nana wasn't always forgiving when someone had scared her half to death. She liked to be in firm control at all times. It was one of her superpowers, as I liked to call them. This had really shaken her, and she was not happy about it.

Hannah knew my grandmother well enough to ignore the comment. She did, however, turn her focus to me. "It must have been vandals. Those statues have been there for years."

"I guess someone got tired of looking at Arthur's pompous face." Nana got up from the couch. "I'm going back to my coffee." She was still mad enough that she didn't even invite Hannah for a cup. I filled in the politeness gap.

"Hannah, can I get you something? Coffee? Or a cup of water?"

Hannah smiled shyly again. "One of those caramel goodies might help relieve some of the anguish I'm feeling."

"Seeing broken statues does not create anguish," Nana called from the kitchen. This time we both ignored her. My grandmother could be prickly when someone upset her.

I winked at Hannah. "I'll get you a caramel bun, but maybe it'll taste better in your own kitchen."

Hannah nodded in agreement.

With Hannah calmed down from her shocking morning and settled in her own kitchen with a caramel roll, I decided to grab my bicycle out of the garage and ride over to the Gramby Estate. I had an hour before I needed to set up for the market, and I was curious to see the headless spectacle.

I pulled my bike out of the corner it had been jammed in for several years. I had no idea why I thought it would be in tiptop shape and ready to race across town. Both tires were flat and cobwebs coated the handlebars and the seat. I rested it back against the wall of the garage and headed out on foot. I'd have less time to spend at the estate, but at least I'd get to see the damage. And who was I kidding? I was hoping to get a glimpse of the manor's newest occupant as well. Maybe he had some insight into what had happened to his ancestor's beloved statues.

It was turning out to be another beautiful, blue sky day in Ripple Creek. There were a few gray thunder clouds nestled on the next peak, but chances were they would eventually coast deeper into the mountain range. I hurried my pace. Laughter rolled up from the creek as I crossed over the bridge. A group of teens had roped together their inner tubes, so they could float down in a big cluster. It was early for a ride down the river, but it was a great way to avoid the crowds. Sometimes the creek could get so packed, inner tubes would get stuck between the banks and cause a traffic jam.

I half expected to see Dalton at the site. After all, there had obviously been some vandalism. Maybe he was still stuck at the resort dealing with their vandalism issues. *Priorities, priorities.*

I was also surprised and a little disappointed that Cade wasn't out on his property inspecting the damage. And damage there was. Each statue had had its head cut clean off. The first statue, the one that used to glower down at you as you reached the top of the garden, had nothing left but a stump of broken, dusty stone where the head once sat. The head, with its dour expression, looked even angrier as it lay in the weeds staring up at the body it once sat upon.

I looked over at the statue with the horse. I'd sat on it enough that I actually felt a little tug of sadness at seeing the rider now as headless as the horseman of Sleepy Hollow. The head had been tossed well clear of the statue. Had the vandal or vandals kicked it around for a bit, like a Flintstone style soccer ball? The third statue on the other end of the garden stood, hands still in pockets, with its own broken neck stump.

A door clicked shut behind me. I spun around. Cade strolled out in a white t-shirt, shorts, a forest green cap and black sunglasses. He was carrying a cup of coffee. He didn't look terribly distraught. He glanced from one statue to the other. "Looks like Arthur had a bad night."

eleven

· · ·

C ade took off his sunglasses and let them dangle from his fingers. "Shouldn't you be out selling cinnamon rolls? I was about to head to town."

"Market doesn't open for another hour and yes, I'll be there with my treats. However, our neighbor, Hannah, interrupted our morning with tales of horror, beheadings and all manner of nightmarish stuff happening at the Gramby Estate."

His hazel eyes looked almost amber in the early morning light. The aroma of coffee drifted toward me as he left the patio and walked my direction. A small flutter in my stomach, different butterflies than the ones that emerged for Dalton, let me know that I had already formed a small crush on Cade. Was that possible? A crush at my age? Maybe it was just gas bubbles. Or maybe not. His aftershave smelled better than the coffee, and I rarely thought anything smelled better than coffee.

"Then I'm sorry I couldn't offer you more than a few broken statues."

"You don't seem too upset that your property has been vandalized. Or did you—?"

"What? Behead the statues myself?" He took a sip of coffee. "Excuse my manners. Would you like a cup? Freshly brewed."

"No, thanks. I've had a cup this morning. One starts my engine. Two makes it idle too high."

He chuckled. "To answer your question, I did not cut off the heads. Granted, Arthur Gramby was not a nice man, and I have heard some unpleasant stories about the guy, but I did not cut off his head." He glanced around. "Or in this case, heads."

"Aren't you the least bit curious what happened? Did you hear anything?"

"I guess I do sound a little cavalier about this, but there's so much to do inside the house, I'm not very concerned about the outside. I assume some teenagers decided it was time to take the old boy down. As for hearing anything, I fell asleep with my headphones on. In my defense, it was a podcast on how to get better sleep."

"Guess it worked then. Do you mind if I look around? I love a good mystery, and the case of Arthur's beheading has me intrigued."

"Go right ahead." His phone rang. He glanced at it. "That's my handyman. He's late again." He walked away to answer it. "Saul, thought you'd be here by now." I heard him say as I crossed the garden to the third, more out of the way, statue. I'd never given it a good look. Arthur must have spent a good deal of money for his stone likenesses. This one was so intricate, I could see the delicate pattern on his waistcoat. A thin watch chain dangled from the pocket. It looked much different without Arthur Gramby's stern expression peering down from the statue.

I tripped on the head as I circled to the back of the statue. It was facedown in the weeds. I didn't need to turn it over to know that there would be a harsh look of disapproval on the face. I peered up to the stump left behind and squinted as sunlight glinted off something shiny. I held Arthur's round shoulders and climbed up on the pedestal at the base of the statue to get a better look. The shiny silver blade of what looked to be a brand new axe was jammed into the stone at the base of the neck, right above the shirt collar.

"Find anything interesting?" Cade called as he approached the statue.

I hopped down from the pedestal. "As a matter of fact, there's a shiny, new axe blade stuck in the stone. The wooden handle has been broken off leaving behind a stump not unlike the stumps left behind on the statues."

Cade was much taller and, therefore, didn't need to climb on the pedestal. He shielded his eyes and stared up at the blade. "Would you look at that? Someone actually went out and bought a brand new axe for his executioner's quest." He stepped back and glanced around at the surrounding grass and weeds. "Do you see the handle? Maybe they left behind some fingerprints."

"I thought you weren't too concerned about catching the culprit," I noted.

"I wasn't. I'm not. Not really. It's just if they went out specially to buy a new ax—"

"Then this was premeditated and not just some wild teenage game of dare."

He shrugged. "Couldn't have said it better myself."

"In that case—do you have any enemies?"

"Where do I start?" Cade chuckled and pulled his glasses down. The sun was getting higher in the sky, and at the high elevation it could be brutally sharp. I was lamenting forgetting my own pair of sunglasses, but I'd left the house in such a hurry, I hadn't thought to put them on.

I was a little perplexed about why a charming man like Cade would have a long list of enemies but then I knew little about the man. Maybe the charm was a façade. I was usually a better judge of character than that. He seemed genuinely likable. "You don't have to tell me. None of my business."

"I'm exaggerating a little, but there are people who would prefer not to see or talk to me. Ex-wife, disgruntled relatives, a literary agent who was so lazy I would have been better represented by a five-year-old, and well, I'll stop there so you don't leave here thinking an ogre just moved into Ripple Creek."

Naturally, the ex-wife was the one mention that got my full attention. "You were married?" It rolled out before I could tell myself not to ask it. "Never mind. Again, none of my business."

"It's all right. Katy and I are actually on speaking terms again. She stays on her side of the country, and I stay on mine. That works out just fine for both of us. Now, back to my headless ancestor—I suppose I should at least mention this to law enforcement. Or maybe Ripple Creek is so small, there is no law enforcement?" He said it as a question.

"We have a ranger, Dalton Braddock. He's a good friend of mine. I think he's up at the Miramont Resort right now, but I could tell him to drop by Gramby Estate on his way down the hill."

"Sure but tell him no emergency. Besides, I won't be home this morning." He smiled. "I've got an appointment to see a woman about her cinnamon rolls."

"Oh! My cinnamon rolls. I need to get to the farmer's market. I'll see you there. Sorry about your statues."

twelve

. . .

Nana had washed down her picturesque cart on wheels. I had no vehicle to transport something so big (an obstacle I hadn't noticed until it came time to pack up for the market) so I filled the cart with my goodies and rolled the whole kit and caboodle to town. It seemed I was leaving a fragrant trail in my wake, and by the time I stopped in front of my sad bakery building and set out my money box, I had a line of customers eager to find out where the aroma was coming from.

The Ripple Creek Farmer's Market was the pride of the community. It had started back when I was a kid when local artists decided they needed a place to display and sell their crafts. People from neighboring towns joined in to sell their goods and buy things. Summer was coming to an end, so the produce was getting scarce. The growing season was short in a mountain climate. If you didn't plant at just the right time, after the last frost, you usually had to wait until the next year to grow vegetables. But some clever people with greenhouses and hydroponic systems managed to supply the market with fresh produce all the way until mid-October when the market shut down until the next spring. The lack of fresh fruits and vegetables didn't put a damper on the market. Halloween and Christmas crafts usually flowed in at the end of summer to fill the void left behind by the veggie farmers. Some of the sellers had rolling carts like mine, and others, who were far more regular to the event, had tents and homemade kiosks to set up. Some booths even had their own logos. Nancy Greenville, who lived on the road past Nana's house, loved to sew little dog and cat outfits. Her animal clothing line was quite popular. Her business had grown since the last time I visited the market. Her teenage sons were still busy putting together the kiosk as people started meandering between the stands.

A pine-scented breeze had flowed into the valley. Many people would be busy trying to keep their banners and light wares from blowing down the street. I had no such problem. Nana had given me her old tin money box, still filled with dollar bills and change. It was solid. I didn't need to worry about it blowing away. The sticky buns were stored safely inside the cart, other than the two I had out on display. I was charging four dollars for each bun.

After an hour of a steady stream of customers, I worried I'd run out long before the end of the market. Everyone seemed pleased with the buns, and some people even came back for seconds. When our local folk band started tuning up their fiddles and guitars, many of the customers flowed in the direction of the small, portable stage. It gave me a chance to count my inventory. If time permitted, I would stop in Esme's bookstore for a chat. She had set up a big easel out front that let everyone know the Nine Lives Bookshop would be open for business next week.

I stooped down and peered into the cart. As I counted, I spotted a pair of brown loafers beneath the cart. Above, I heard a man speaking angrily. Since no one responded, I surmised he was on the phone. I felt somewhat weird about popping up into the middle of what sounded like a tense conversation, so I stayed crouched for a minute while he finished up.

"I've told you, Saul, I need that money. I'm going to start piling on interest if I don't get it soon." His rant ended. I used that as my opportunity to stand up. I'd been crouched down long enough that I momentarily felt lightheaded.

"Didn't see you down there." His tone was much more jovial now. He was a fifty-something man with dark gray hair and long sideburns. It was a warm summer day, and one didn't normally see a suit, an ill-fitting one at that, at the farmer's market. His was brown with heavy stitching to accentuate the pockets and trim. His tie had bright yellow flowers on a dark pink background. "You're new here, aren't you?" he asked.

"Yes and no. I grew up in Ripple Creek. I recently moved

back to open a bakery." I pointed unenthusiastically at the brick building behind me.

"Oh, right, I think Jason from our realty office sold that old bakery. I'm Kent Milner, from Milner Realty, by the way. Guess I'm looking at the buyer. Don't worry. A few splashes of paint and some new flooring, and the place will shine like a jewel." It was realtor doublespeak for you bought yourself a fixer-upper.

"It might take a little more than that, but I'm excited to get started. Now, what can I get you? We've got two choices, traditional cinnamon with a sugary glaze and caramel and pecan. I must warn you the latter will require some finger licking." I pointed out my cinnamon and caramel examples.

"Gosh, I'll take one of each. Not both for me, of course." He patted his round belly that was working the buttons on his coat to capacity. "The wife would not be happy if she smelled cinnamon on me, and I didn't bring her one too."

I set to work plucking out a plump cinnamon and caramel roll. Part of the conversation I'd overheard contained the name Saul. I was curious to know if it was the Saul who supposedly fixes all, the handyman Cade had hired to spruce up the estate. Kent seemed friendly enough. I decided he wouldn't mind me asking.

"I'm ashamed to admit I overheard your phone conversation while I was crouched down counting my inventory. I heard you mention the name Saul. Is that the same Saul as the handyman in the white van?" Maybe I'd made a mistake. He grimaced at the question.

"Don't remind me of that man when I'm about to eat a sweet treat."

"I'm sorry. I was just curious because my friend hired him to work on his estate."

"Yes, the Gramby Estate. I don't know why Mr. Rafferty hired him. Saul never gets the work done. He's lazy and greedy. You see, Saul Bonelli is my brother-in-law. My wife would be mad at me for talking about him like this, but if Rafferty is your friend, you might warn him. Tell him what I said. Saul will only cause him headaches, and, in between that, he'll bleed him dry."

"Oh dear, I'll let my friend know." I handed him his rolls, and he gave me his cash. "Enjoy the treats."

"I plan to." He paused and turned back around, fishing in his pocket for something. "If you have any more realty needs, give me a call."

"Thanks, I will." He strolled away with his rolls, managing to stop and talk to just about everyone in his path and making sure to hand each person a business card before he walked away.

I was torn over whether I should let Cade know about Saul's business practices. First of all, was my source reliable and unbiased? It seemed Saul owed Kent some money, and he was plenty angry about the debt. Was that clouding his opinion of his brother-in-law? Was it my place to tell Cade who he should and shouldn't hire to work on his property? It seemed altogether too personal considering we'd known each other less than a day. Then again, I might be doing Cade a big favor, which, in turn, might solidify our friendship. I wouldn't mind that at all. One thing I'd found about living in a small, secluded town like Ripple Creek, you couldn't have too many friends. I'd have to give it some thought, but I was leaning in the direction of putting out a mild warning about his handyman.

thirteen

. . .

I'd set aside a traditional cinnamon roll, one of the plumper ones with a good coating of glaze, for Cade. It was a good thing I had because I sold out of rolls an hour before the market shut down. I let disappointed customers, many who were back for seconds, know that I'd be returning the following week with a new treat. I'd have to start an actual plan for getting the bakery open so I had something more succinct to tell people other than eventually I'll be opening a bakery in the building behind me. *Eventually* just wasn't going to cut it. I'd have a better idea on the timeline once I spoke to Dalton's friend, Mike. My only concern was that he'd be too far booked out. There was a lot of new construction going on at the bottom of the highway. Of course, there was always Saul. Apparently, he could fix all. I'd made a solid decision to let Cade know what I'd heard about his handyman. Kent had an obvious bias against his brother-in-law, and it all seemed to stem from a money issue. Still, it would be good to warn Cade while at the same time adding in the caveat that Kent Milner was definitely not on good terms with his brother-in-law.

Esme popped out of her shop and headed over to my cart. "I've been nibbling on that caramel bun all morning. I wanted the experience to last, so I was taking small bites at a time. So good. I can't wait until the bakery is open. I'll have to start taking exercise classes to counteract the huge amounts of calories I plan to consume."

Esme looked like one of those tall, thin runway models. I shot her an annoyed brow raise. "As a person who has to take into account every bite I eat, I'm going to go out on a limb and say that you have never had to count calories or bites or, for that matter, cinnamon rolls."

Esme smiled coyly and tucked her short hair behind her ears. "Actually, that's not true. I had to count calories, only not in the way you mean."

I nodded. "Aha, so you had to be fed high calorie foods as a kid just to keep from disappearing when you turned sideways."

"Something like that. Believe me, it was not fun. For awhile, my mom started making mashed potatoes and gravy with every meal, and she made me eat a bowl of that first."

"I'm going to leave the sorrowful violin tune off the table for now because most of us, growing up, would have eaten mashed potatoes and gravy for breakfast, lunch and dinner if offered."

"Maybe that wasn't the best example." Esme looked past me. "Wow, who is that? Not too shabby."

I twisted back to look in the same direction. Cade had stopped at the first kiosk in the line of sellers. Kelli Hobgarten sold flavor infused olive oils. She was extra gregarious with her current customer. I could hear her tinny sounding laugh all the way down to my cart.

"That's Cade Rafferty," I told Esme. "He's a writer, and he's moved into his ancestor's home on the Gramby Estate."

"The Gramby Estate? Is that the old stone mansion with the kind of creepy looking statues in the garden?"

"Yes, and if you thought they were creepy before wait until you see them now."

"What do you mean? Oops, never mind. It looks like he's heading this way."

"Don't tell me I'm too late." Cade's deep, sort of chiding tone was already familiar.

I stuck on a Cheshire Cat grin as I stooped down and emerged with the cinnamon roll. "I just happen to have one left with your name on it. Not literally, of course. I saved it for you—just in case you were able to pull yourself away from your computer."

Cade grinned down at the roll on the plate. "So it's true— it does help to have friends in high places."

I shrugged. "I do live at eight thousand feet elevation, so I guess that works. Cade, this is my friend, Esme. She owns that fabulous looking bookstore behind us."

Esme stuck out her hand. "Nice to meet you. Cade Rafferty," she repeated, then snapped her fingers. "You wrote *Dark*

Towers. I loved that one, but I had to keep the hallway light on for a week."

"Then my mission was accomplished." Cade nodded politely. "I'm honored to meet you."

I was going to have to start reading gothic thrillers. "Taste the roll," I said, deciding to break up the little exchange of compliments. It seemed I was still stuck in my teenage years. Hopefully, that would wear off soon.

Cade took a bite and did the whole taste test thing with furrowed brows and moving the bite around from cheek to cheek to get the full experience. He finally swallowed with great flourish. "Delicious."

I released the breath I hadn't realized I'd been holding until it rushed out of my lungs.

"I've got to get back to the store. I still have a lot of books to shelve." Esme smiled at Cade. "Including some of the illustrious Cade Rafferty's books." Her eyes rounded, and she sucked in a sharp breath. "Do you think you'd ever consider doing a book signing in my shop?"

Cade seemed flattered, albeit reluctant, about the suggestion. "Uh, sure, but my newest book is still half up here." He tapped the side of his head. "Maybe when it's released we can talk about a book signing."

Esme put her hand to her chest. "I can't tell you how much that would mean to me and my humble little bookstore." She was certainly acting the coquette. Not the no-nonsense woman I'd met on our first encounter. Who could blame her? Cade did have that certain something.

Esme returned to her bookshop. Cade stuck around my

now officially empty cart and ate his cinnamon roll. "Hmm, really good," he said as he finished the last bite. He looked over at me with one eye squinted shut. "Are you going to make cherry Danish when you open your shop? They're my favorite."

"I'll put them on the list. It's easy enough to make a variety of Danish as long as you have the flaky dough prepared. I must warn you that I'm planning to put a vintage edge on most of my creations. I hope to win hearts, minds and tastebuds with bouts of nostalgia and dollops of frosting."

"That should be your motto." He held up his hand as if reading the words in the sky. "Come in for the nostalgia, leave with a dollop of frosting. Or something like that. My word-smithing has been off all morning. I wrote the same chapter twice and then immediately deleted it. I think it's because my patio table is now surrounded by headless statues. By the way, I put in a call to Ranger Braddock. He's still up at the ski resort, but he says he'll stop by later."

"You might as well get him to look at the damage, so he can make a report. How is the new handyman working out?" I decided to get a feeling for his opinion on Saul before I blurted out what I'd heard.

"He might be another reason for my twice deleted chapter. Aside from the noise he's making with his chainsaw—he decided it was the best way to tackle some of the overgrown landscape—he takes an awful lot of breaks and phone calls. Not entirely sure he's going to work out. It's just hard to get anyone up here."

"I agree. Nana and I once walked around in three layers of clothes and socks because our furnace was broken. We practically had to beg a heat and air guy to come up the hill. I hate to throw salt on that wound, but I spoke with Saul's brother-in-law, Kent Milner, today. He's a realtor and, from what I gathered, not one of Saul's biggest fans. He said Saul is lazy and greedy and not to be trusted."

"I was beginning to get that feeling from him. So far I only have him clearing landscape. I don't think he can mess that up too much. However, if there's little progress, then I'm going to pay what I owe him and send him and his shambling, sputtering van on their way."

"I hope, for your sake, that he at least delivers on his landscape clearing. What will you do about the statues?"

Cade brushed some of his hair back with his fingers. He certainly had a thick head of it. "I'm not sure if they're more or less disconcerting without their heads. Honestly, I was planning to have them lifted and hauled into the old carriage house for storage. Now, I might just have them ground down and hauled away as rocks and rubble. You don't happen to know anyone who specializes in old statue removal?"

I laughed. "I don't have anyone like that on speed dial. However, I have heard about this guy named Saul. Apparently he fixes all."

Cade smiled. "I like you, Ramone." He wadded up the napkin and placed it in the paper bag I'd brought for trash. "And I really like your cinnamon rolls." (Ha, take that bookseller with your vast knowledge of books). Cade stretched up and looked around at the other booths. "Nope, I don't need anything else. I really just came here to see you... and to procrastinate from my work."

I was trying not to let the notion that he came to the market to see me go to my head. But it was hard. Especially after the month I'd had. "Procrastination, she's a fickle one. I've become far too acquainted with her these past weeks. But now I'm kicking her to the curb. People liked my rolls. I need to go home and start that list of baked goods. I'll be sure to add cherry Danish."

"Yes, success. Now my trip to town was doubly worth it. I'll see you later, Ramone."

I lingered for a second to watch him stroll away. It wasn't quite like watching Dalton walk off on his horse, but it was good. Good in a different way, and maybe that needed to be my new focus. Making my life different in every way.

fourteen

. . .

The cart had moved easier when it was filled with my baked goods. Empty, it managed to bump and hop and jump wildly over every small obstacle in the road. By the time I reached home, I was glad to be rid of the thing. I gave it a nice shove, and it rolled into the garage. My bicycle had been pulled out from its corner. Nana had washed it and pumped up the tires.

I headed inside. "Nana, I thought you might make it to the market."

Nana leaned her head into the kitchen doorway. She was wearing a tie-dyed apron. "Too hot outside. How did it go? I've made you a grilled cheese with gouda and Swiss, the way you like it."

"You're the best. I'm starving. I had so many customers I never had time to take a break." Nana handed me a plate with a golden toasted sandwich bursting with soft melted cheese.

"Keep this up, and you'll never get me out of your painting studio."

Nana returned from the refrigerator with a pitcher of lemonade. "You know I love taking care of you, Button. Just like when you were growing up. Only I know *you* need to get back out there as an adult." She poured us each a glass and sat down across from me. "You were too busy to take a break? I assume that means the morning went well."

"Very well. I'm going to spend the afternoon brainstorming a list of baked goods. There are a lot of things that need to be taken into account to put together a good menu. I need to talk to Roxi. I'm hoping she has a few good wholesalers to work with. I have to figure out a schedule so that everything bakes in time for when the first customers walk inside. A good bakery has to run like a well-oiled machine. I'll have to be in the shop by three in the morning."

Nana sat back stunned. "Three in the morning?"

"How else will I get sourdoughs proofed, cakes frosted and pastries baked?"

"I suppose that makes sense. You'll need an assistant. I could help until you find someone."

I covered her hand with mine. "Thanks, Nana. I'll advertise before I even open the doors. I doubt there's anyone local. I'll have to offer a good salary and benefits to get someone to move up to Ripple Creek." I waved off that worry. "But that's still in the future. First, I have to get a contractor to look at the place. Dalton's friend is coming up here on Friday. My only worry is that his calendar will be booked."

"Then we'll find a different contractor. It doesn't have to be Dalton's friend." Nana said as if it was an easy thing to do.

"We're in a location that's not exactly brimming with tradespeople, Nana. But that's all right. In the meantime, I'll sell my goods at the street fair until it ends in fall."

Nana frowned. "But what about winter? It's going to be much harder getting the work done in the dead of winter."

"Gosh, I hadn't thought about that. I'll figure something out." I savored a few good bites of my sandwich. "Hmm, this is exactly what I needed, Nana. And I saw you cleaned my bicycle."

"Yep and I put air in the tires."

"Thanks so much. Oh, and I went to see the Gramby statues. Hannah was right. It was a massacre."

"Who would do such a thing? Those three statues have been sitting up at that site for more than a century. Why now?"

"Cade couldn't think of any reason for it."

Nana smiled slyly. "Cade is it? You two are on first name terms."

"Well, since calling each other Mr. Rafferty and Miss Ramone is nineteenth-century awkward, yes, we're on first name terms." I finished half my sandwich but like when I was young and I had something exciting on my mind, I had a hard time sitting still to eat. "I'll save this other half for later. I want to get started brainstorming."

"No need to leave the lunch table." Nana got up and walked to the kitchen drawer that contained everything except stuff that belonged in a kitchen. She pulled out a notepad and pen and set it down next to me.

"Perfect." I wiped my hands and picked up the pen. "You're going to be one of my sources for all things vintage."

"Gee, thanks for that."

I laughed. "You know what I mean. What kind of baked treats do you remember growing up? What goodies hold a particular piece of your heart? Maybe something your mom made for holidays or your birthday."

Nana's laugh was not one of humor. "You're talking about you great-grandmother Mabel. Better known to me as Attila the Hun. She wasn't exactly the baking type, and since she kicked me and, technically, your mom out before I reached my sixteenth birthday, I hardly have fond memories of her in the kitchen."

I grimaced at my mistake. "I'm sorry, Nana. That was a thoughtless question. It's just I had such a wonderful upbringing here with you in Ripple Creek, I forget how rough you had it."

"That's all right. I hadn't given her a second of thought in years. However, I did love my Granny Tootsie. That's what we called her."

"You said she died when you were ten."

"That's right. I used to spend summers at her little farm-stead in Kansas. Now, *she* knew how to bake." She sat back and closed her eyes, taking herself back to that time on Granny Tootsie's farm. "Let's see. She'd always make peanut butter fingers. At least that's what we called them because they were shaped like fingers. And she dipped one end in melted chocolate. I always saved that end for last."

"Finger shaped cookies were popular back then." I wrote down peanut butter fingers. I could add my own edge with thick dark chocolate and chopped peanuts.

"In summer, when the rhubarb was growing like weeds, she'd make strawberry, rhubarb hand pies. Fruity goodness tucked in a neat little purse of buttery pastry. Those were delicious. I can still remember sitting out on her back stoop with a little pie in my hand. She had this pushy hen named Etta. That bird would walk up and down those steps, stopping at the top one every time to look me straight in the eye, trying to intimidate me into sharing my pie."

"See, those are the goodies I want in my bakery. I don't want to just serve tasty treats. I want to serve up sentimental time travel. I want people to eat my treats and be taken back to fond childhood memories."

"I think that's a wonderful idea, Button. Sour cream jumbles. Tootsie used to make these delicate round cinnamon cookies. She said the secret ingredient was fresh sour cream."

I wrote it down.

"And on my birthday, she'd make me a fluffy white angel food cake covered in strawberry frosting." I'd taken Nana back to the carefree days on her grandmother's farm. We'd had to jump over the unpleasant chunk of time in between, the time with her mother, but now she was fully immersed.

I wrote down angel food cake. "I wonder if I could create some angel food cupcakes or small individual cakes that I could top with pillowy clouds of marshmallow frosting."

"This brainstorming is giving me a sweet tooth," Nana noted.

As I wrote down my angel food idea, sirens shattered the otherwise quiet afternoon. Nana got up and went to the window. "Looks like they're heading across the bridge. It's an ambulance and a fire truck."

I got up to join her at the window. Naturally, we expected the vehicles with their spinning red lights to turn east toward town. Instead, they went west toward the Gramby Estate.

"Oh no. Something must have happened at the estate. This time it looks far more serious than statues being vandalized." I spun around and grabbed my cap and sunglasses. "Guess it's time to try out my newly restored bicycle. I sure hope nothing's happened to Cade."

fifteen

· · ·

I pedaled like a madwoman toward the Gramby Estate. My teeth clattered together as I rode over the planks on the bridge. The creek below was packed with people floating along on inner tubes. A few of the more agile creek riders had pulled their tubes off the water to climb the steep banks and get a look at whatever was going on at the big stone house across the way. Up ahead, squirrels were dashing into trees to get away from the red flashing ruckus traveling up the usually quiet road.

The long fire truck waddled side to side as it made its way up the gravel path to the house. The ambulance was already parked next to Saul's van, and two paramedics were pulling a gurney and gear out of the back. My heart was racing not just from the bike ride but from the possibility that something terrible had happened to Cade. None of the emergency crews paid any attention to the woman on the bicycle. My newly pumped tires had taken me as far as possible. I laid it down in the tall grass and made my way toward the house. Cade was alone in Ripple Creek. If he had taken ill or had an accident, I was sure a friendly face would be a comfort.

I was so relieved when I saw Cade walking out to meet the ambulance crew I nearly clapped and cheered. The expression on Cade's face assured me something quite serious had taken place. The paramedics and a fireman followed Cade around the side of the house to his back patio area. I glanced back toward the bridge to see if Dalton was joining the rest of the team, but there was no sign of him. It seemed Ripple Creek might be getting the short end of the stick on law enforcement now that he was to marry into the Miramont family.

I hurried across the overgrown landscape, working hard not to get caught up in a mass of bindweed or trip over a clump of dandelions. Two robins, who'd been busy snatching worms from the ground, fluttered up in front of me, causing me to stumble back a few steps. My legs felt slightly wobbly as I moved my feet forward again. I'd had more exercise in the past few days than in the entire last month combined. Living in Ripple Creek was going to require a little more muscle and fitness than living in the city. I was all for it.

I circled the house, unsure of what to expect on the other side. I sensed it wasn't going to be anything as minor as the statue beheading. I found Cade standing a good distance back from his patio. His table and chairs seemed to be the center of everyone's attention. As one of the paramedics stepped to the side, I caught a glimpse of what they were looking at. Saul was slumped over Cade's patio table. He had on the green cap I'd seen Cade wearing in the morning. There was a pitcher half full of tea on the table. An empty glass lay on its side, resting against the top of Saul's shoulder. One of his arms was on the table, and one hung limply at his side.

I reached where Cade was standing. He glanced over, slightly startled. "It's you, Scottie. I thought it might be—" He stopped, apparently deciding it was better not to finish the sentence.

"It might be?" I asked to remind him where he left off. Then it dawned on me. "Wait, was Saul, you know, murdered?"

"There's a hole in the back of his head that would make it a likely possibility. And then there was the gunshot." Cade seemed only minimally distressed by it all. I'd already learned that about him. His feathers didn't ruffle easily. Maybe it was because his imagination was always chock-full with intrigue and murder.

"You heard a gunshot?" Now *I* was intrigued. I'd helped solve the murder of Nana's very unpleasant neighbor, and I had to admit the sleuthing bug had caught me. Now, it seemed I'd have a chance to test out my investigative skills again. And with Dalton always busy up on the hill, it seemed the town might just need me. At least that was what I was going to tell myself.

On closer look, Cade did seem a little off his usual level of confidence. "It happened at 1:13. I was inside. I've made a small office for myself in an alcove off the main room. The sun was too hot and bright to work out on the table and Saul had been making so much noise, I moved my laptop inside. I heard a sharp bang. It took me a second to figure out what it was, but the reverberation and the sound was definitely from a gun. I glanced at the time on my computer. Habit, I guess. At first, I brushed it off as someone doing target practice. Sound carries so much in this valley, I figured the shot could have been fired from miles away. I was finally on a roll with my writing for the day, so I finished a paragraph and then realized I hadn't heard Saul's chainsaw for at least fifteen minutes. The man rested more than he worked. I thought I'd head outside and nudge him to get started again."

Cade looked toward the patio table. "I guess he sat down to the pitcher of tea I'd left out. He even pulled on my cap to shade himself while he took a break. I actually considered that he might be sleeping when I first saw him draped over the table. I walked over to shake him awake and let him know I wasn't paying him for a nap. That was when I saw that the hair on the back of his head was matted with blood. On closer inspection, I spotted the bullet hole."

"That's horrific. Are you all right? Must have been quite a shock."

"I think I'm still in that state of shock. I'm sure it'll hit me later." He shook his head. "I thought I could come up here, get away from distractions and get this book finished. Now, it seems my back patio has become a crime scene."

One of the paramedics was on his phone as he walked toward us. His grim expression told us what we already knew. Saul Bonelli was dead.

"Mr. Rafferty, I've just informed Ranger Braddock of

what's happened on your property. He'll be here soon." That pronouncement sent a little flutter through me, but I'd mostly managed to get over my overreaction to seeing Dalton. "As you've probably already concluded, the victim is dead. Since it appears he died from a gunshot to the back of the head, there'll have to be a full investigation. We've contacted the county coroner. The team will be here as soon as they can get up the mountain. In the meantime, we're needed elsewhere, so we'll be on our way."

"Thank you for getting here so fast."

The paramedic headed back to the others. We stood together watching as the emergency vehicles withdrew from the property. A clump of clouds had rolled in adding some intermittent shadows to the macabre scene.

"I'll stay with you until Dalton gets here," I said.

"Dalton? Oh, right, the ranger. You mentioned you were friends." Cade was slowly peeling back the layer of shock. He was still holding it together well, but this had shaken him. Who could blame him? I was feeling shaken, and it wasn't even my property. "What a day. First, the vandalism and now a murder, an actual murder. I write about this stuff all the time, but those crimes are all fiction, mere figments of my imagination. Seeing a real one, up close and at my own home, is a whole different matter. I really appreciate you sticking around. Not too sure what to make of all this."

"Do you think it's connected to the statue destruction?" I asked.

"I'm not sure. It's awfully coincidental if the two are not related."

Something occurred to me. "Cade, what if this wasn't murder? What if some teens or some adult was out doing target practice somewhere in the wilderness, and a bullet strayed this way."

"And just happened to hit Saul directly in the back of the head? I'd say the odds are against it, but you never know. When you fire a gun, the bullet has to land somewhere. It won't do Saul any good, but I hope you're right. An accidental death is less scary than a murder."

sixteen

. . .

We had the crime scene to ourselves while we waited for the coroner to come up the mountain and the ranger to come down.

"I suppose this is what living in a small, remote town is like. You've got a dead body on your patio, and there's no one available to take it away," Cade said. We'd gone inside to get glasses of water. The oak kitchen cabinets had been bleached nearly to the color of pine from wear and time. One or two doors seemed to be hanging on a single hinge. The soapstone kitchen counter and adjacent work table were scarred from use as well. Veins of green spliced through the otherwise chalky black stone. A little mineral oil and it would shine like new. That was the beauty of soapstone.

"You're lucky this happened in summer," I noted. "That's probably not the right phrase since it's not the least bit lucky, but in winter, you might have been staring at the dead body for a few days." I glanced out the kitchen window. I should have been repelled by the sight and probably would have been if it had been more gruesome death, but I was intrigued. I wanted badly to know what had happened to Saul Bonelli. Cade and I had placated our deepest fears for a moment and entertained the idea that it was merely a stray bullet from someone's round of target practice. Poor Saul had been unlucky enough to stop the bullet with his head. But we both knew that was probably not the case. I drank the rest of the water and placed the glass in the sink.

"You don't have to join me, but I'm going to look around. If this was murder, then maybe the killer left some evidence behind."

"Are you kidding? I'd love to join you on an evidence hunt. Intrigue is my middle name." He smiled. "Not really."

"Yes, I had an inkling that was rhetorical."

The earlier clouds had thickened, and a breeze had come with them to push them farther over the mountain. They dropped shadows over the patio. The green cap was still on Saul's head. The bill was pressed under his forehead keeping it secure even in the wind. The bullet hole and resulting blood were just below the back edge of the cap. We both stood silently for a second, contemplating how quickly life could end. In the midst of our thoughtful reflection, we both came to the same startling conclusion.

"It was me," Cade said darkly at the same time that I blurted "it was you".

"Makes sense. He was wearing my green hat and sitting

at my table." Cade was a little less held together than earlier in the afternoon. "The killer came up from behind, took the shot and left thinking they'd killed their intended target. Me." He pulled out a chair before I could remind him not to touch anything at the crime scene. His legs gave out halfway to the seat. "It's obvious. Someone was trying to kill me."

"I know I've asked you about enemies before, but do you have any idea who it might be?"

Cade put his elbow on the table and rubbed his forehead with his thumb and forefinger. "Like I said, there are a few people out there who are irritated with me, but I can't think of anyone who'd want to kill me. Although, clearly, I'm wrong about that."

He was understandably distressed by the notion.

"Hold on. Before you start getting too upset about it, we might be wrong. After all, Saul is much shorter and rounder in his proportions. And he has gray in his hair. Other than the hat, you don't look anything alike. Also, he's wearing coveralls. If it was a case of mistaken identity, the killer sure didn't pay attention to detail. I haven't known you long, but I'd bet a hundred bucks that you have never pulled on a pair of coveralls in your life."

"You'd win that bet." A slight grin returned to his face. He was absorbing and, once again, dealing confidently with the prospect of someone trying to kill him.

"If it was someone you knew, one of your perceived enemies, then they would know that the man sitting in grass stained coveralls was not Cade Rafferty."

"Unless this was just some madman out for a random killing," Cade added.

"You spend far too much time in your fictional worlds."

"Guilty as charged. But let's face it. There are a lot of whack jobs out there."

"Agreed." I walked around and stood behind Saul, then turned to walked in what I considered a fairly straight line from the back of his head. The garden was so lush and over-grown, it was easy enough to spot footprints by looking for smashed grass and weeds. Most of the heavy imprints came from every direction and congregated around the patio. That made sense considering there were two paramedics and three firemen standing in the exact location just fifteen minutes earlier. It seemed clear I wasn't going to find any ta-da moments in the grass. I turned back to the body. His head wound was neat, almost perfect like the shape of a bullet.

Cade pushed up from the chair. "Find anything interesting, Ramone?"

"No, but I was thinking—the bullet hole is neat. There wasn't a lot of damage."

"The weapon couldn't have been anything treacherous like an assault rifle. It must have come from a good distance away," he stated what I was already thinking.

"A hunting rifle and a hunter with very good aim."

"Good work, Ramone."

I didn't mind him always calling me Ramone. For one, I was fond of my last name and not just because it was attached to a famous rock band. I always thought it was a cool name, and his use of it let me know that we were already buddies.

"Can you remember anything else about those fatal moments? Aside from the gunshot, did you happen to hear a vehicle? This place is rather remote compared to the rest of the town. It seems highly possible that the killer came here in some kind of vehicle."

Cade rubbed the stubble on his chin in thought. "I would have heard if a car or truck had pulled up to the site." He snapped his fingers. "Come to think of it, a few minutes before the gunshot, I was concentrating on my work, trying to come up with a clever piece of dialog when a noise interrupted my thoughts. It was somewhere in the distance, but it sounded like a loud bumble bee. The sound brought back a memory. When I was fifteen, my grandfather bought me a dirt bike to ride around on his property. It sounded a lot like that, like the buzz of a dirt bike. The gunshot erased it from my mind, but now that I've come out of the fog left behind by this whole bizarre day, I remember it. Definitely a dirt bike."

"People do use those to ride around on some of the less traveled trails." I headed toward the stretch of gravel leading up from the road. Cade followed with interest.

"The ground is hard and dry from the long summer, but the gravel—" I pointed to a section where the gravel had been disturbed, almost split like the proverbial Red Sea. "That looks like a tire track."

Cade pointed out the same disturbance in the gravel on the other side of the path. "Two tires," he said. "That was probably the moving truck or even the fire truck. Dirt bikes kick up plenty of dust, but I don't think they'd make that kind of dent in gravel. Besides, I think the noise I heard came more from the northeast, from the wilderness on that side of the property. This house is surrounded by so many trees and shrubs it would be easy enough for someone to hide out there."

"Good work, Rafferty." I *high-fived* back with a grin instead of the usual hand slap.

"Guess we're both still learning this detective stuff."

"Looks that way. I think I'll have a look around the garden, just in case."

Cade looked at his phone. "Darn, I've got a conference call with my editor. He's checking on my progress." He rolled his eyes. "Like having my mom double check my division home-work. Anyhow, feel free to look around. I'm going to head inside and let him know what's happened. Should be a good enough excuse for a little more time."

"All right. I'm sure Ranger Braddock will be here soon, as well."

Cade went back inside. I decided to head back to the first crime scenes, the various vandalized statues. It would sure be a big coincidence if both events happened on the same day but were entirely unconnected. I stopped at the center statue, the one that used to greet me with a sour expression as I reached the top of the garden. Other than the broken off head, there was no evidence left behind. I wasn't exactly sure what I was looking for, but something told me I'd know it if I saw it.

I stood for a brief, impromptu memorial at the headless statue on the horse. It had, after all, been a part of my childhood. As an adult and seeing it destroyed as it was, I felt a touch of shame about how often I'd climbed up to play on it. In my defense, it was a life-size horse and one that you didn't need to know how to ride. It was fun to imagine myself galloping across fields on the easy to manage steed.

The earlier patch of clouds that had lent a somewhat sinister array of shadows to the estate had moved on without a sprinkle of rain or flash of lightning. It was late enough in the summer that the threat of afternoon thunderstorms was long over. It seemed the remainder of the afternoon would be pleasant and sunny. I strolled across the grass and weed patches toward the third statue on the opposite side of the garden. Saul's chainsaw was sitting next to a heavily over-grown shrub at the top of the steps. There were a few piles of newly cut debris, but it seemed Cade had not exaggerated. Saul had not gotten much done.

The third statue still contained the one major piece of evidence, the axe blade. It was wedged deeply into the stone. I circled around the statue to get a better look at it. A breeze rolled through the massive clearing where the house and garden sat. As I peered up at the axe blade, something flut-tered against my leg. I startled thinking it might be a bee or wasp. It was a piece of paper. I bent down and picked it up. It was a receipt from our local sporting goods store. The store carried tools and gardening supplies in the back room. The customer who'd dropped the receipt had purchased only one item—a wood-splitting axe. I stuck the receipt in my pocket. I wasn't sure if it would help with the murder case, but it abso-lutely had something to do with the vandalism.

I'd caught the sleuthing bug again. I glanced over toward the patio. The green cap stayed stubbornly on Saul's head.

I was ready to go full in on this one, but there was no denying it was a tough case. Mostly due to one big question. Who was the intended victim?

seventeen

. . .

Cade came back outside after only a few minutes. He handed me a glass of iced tea. "I don't have much in the kitchen. I'm embarrassed to say I have some of those waxy store-bought mini donuts. I'm especially embarrassed to admit it after tasting your cinnamon roll."

"The tea is plenty." I took a long sip. Investigating had left me parched. "Did you really like my cinnamon roll?"

"It was perfect. The right amount of cinnamon and sugary glaze. Find anything of note? By the way, Ranger Braddock called me just after I finished with my editor. He didn't believe me at first, my editor, not Braddock. He thought I was making it up, you know, like the whole dog ate my homework scenario. I told him I could walk outside to my patio and take a picture of the dead man with a hole in his head if he needed proof. He decided to take my word for it. Anyhow, the ranger said the coroner should be here any minute. Braddock was held up by some kind of car accident, where the two drivers got out on the highway and started a fist fight. He's just cleaning up that mess, then he'll be here. He said it was best for the coroner to get a head start."

"Dalton sure has his hands full. He transferred up here because he needed a break from the chaos in the city. I don't think he's getting much of a reprieve." I reached into my pocket and pulled out the receipt from the sporting goods store. "I found this over by statue number three." I nodded toward the statue on the far side of the garden.

Cade unraveled it. "Hmm, looks like our statue executioner shopped at the local sporting goods store for his axe. Too bad he lost the receipt. He'll never get his money back now," he quipped.

I put the receipt back in my pocket. "I'm wondering about Saul's next of kin. I met his brother-in-law. I'm sure his sister will be distraught. I wonder if Saul had a wife."

Cade nodded once. "That I can help you with. Saul was big on chatting. I guess it kept him from having to work while I paid him his thirty dollars an hour. He said he'd never been married. He said"—Cade looked pointedly at me—"and these are his words, not mine—'women only want your money and your time, and I don't have enough of either to spare.'" Cade nodded again. "End quote."

"That means his sister might be the only next of kin. She'll have to be told before word gets around town."

"I think that falls into Ranger Braddock's lap, telling the

next of kin." In the distance, tires rumbled over the bridge. Dust and a few birds taking off from nearby trees let us know the coroner's van had arrived. Cade and I watched as it moved slowly, cautiously up the gravel road.

"He's driving as if he has nitroglycerin in the back of the van," Cade noted.

"Your driveway is a little rough. I'll let you talk to the coroner since this is your house. I'm going to snoop around Saul's van and see if there's anything interesting inside."

Cade whipped a napkin out of his pocket. "I brought this for handling important evidence." He winked as he handed it to me.

"Good thinking. Guess I really am a newbie at this." The coroner's van reached the top of the gravel path. Everything past that was tall grass and wilderness. The team would have to carry their equipment and roll the gurney through the unkempt garden.

As Cade waited to lead the coroner and his assistant to the crime scene, I wandered off to look for evidence. If Saul was the intended victim, and there was still a question about that, then his van might give me some clues into his life. I pulled out the napkin and held it as I tugged on the door handle. I was in luck. The door was unlocked. I opened the driver's side. Instantly, the smell of cigars struck me. A metal lunch pail sat on the passenger's seat. There were granola bar and beef jerky wrappers littering the floor of the van. An interesting and somewhat contrasting duo of snack choices. Along with the wrappers, there were empty soda cans and a tube of sunblock. Nothing that I wouldn't expect to see in Saul's van. I leaned in and looked between the seats to the cargo section of the vehicle. It was piled haphazardly with tools and gardening supplies. Saul had not exactly been a neat and orderly handyman.

The lunch pail looked a little sad sitting in the late afternoon sun, seemingly aware that it wouldn't be used again. I wondered if Saul had eaten his lunch before he was killed. I reached across and, carefully, with napkin in hand, opened the latch and lifted the lid. Saul's sandwich, ham and cheese, sat untouched in the lunch pail. Next to it something was bundled in a napkin. The napkin had some print and a logo. I doubted it would be significant, but if Saul was the intended victim it would be good to know what places he frequented. I felt a little guilty unwrapping his treat. The poor guy would never get to enjoy it. Two butter cookies were wrapped inside. The napkin came from Castillo's Deli. It was a popular eating place up near the Miramont Resort. Before I wrapped the cookies back up, I noticed that someone had handwritten a note to go along with the cookies. "To my Honeybear. Love, Bunny." Saul might have had a philosophy about women just wanting money and time, but it seemed he'd had a sweetheart. I snapped a quick picture of the napkin and wrapped the cookies up before setting them back in the lunch pail. I closed the latch and left the box just as I had found it on the passenger seat. I decided not to let Dalton know I'd been snooping around.

More tires thumped over the bridge. From my vantage point, high up on the property, I could see Dalton's truck crossing the bridge. I closed the door quickly and did a little double check of my face and hair in the side view mirror of the van. I groaned at the sight staring back at me and reminded myself, just as quickly, that it didn't matter. Dalton Braddock was as good as married.

eighteen

. . .

It seemed I was to be the liaison between Dalton and the town's newest resident. Both men, oddly enough, seemed to be sizing each other up as Cade and I walked down to meet the ranger. Dalton looked frazzled and a little sunburned from his day up the mountain. I knew he'd been conducting some sort of overnight stakeout to catch vandals up at the resort. The day had only grown longer and more filled with problems. I was sure a murder was the last thing he wanted to deal with after a nearly twenty-four hour shift. Still, I probably shouldn't have acted quite so chummy when we reached him. (Of course, he had seen me in merely a t-shirt and ratty hair the morning before, so that would qualify as chummy.)

My big mistake started with a comment. "Dalton, you look like you need a nap."

His glower struck me like a slap. "I'm fine." His response

was so curt, it was like another slap. I'd said entirely the wrong thing, and now I'd embarrassed myself in front of Cade. Cade immediately tensed up next to me.

"Cade Rafferty," he said coldly. His hand shot out. Dalton shook it.

"Ranger Braddock." The two men still seemed to be sizing each other up like a couple of bulls placed in the same pen. "I see the coroner is still here. I'll get the briefing from him and then you can give me your statement." He strode past with his shoulders held rigid.

I stayed behind with Cade. I was feeling about as hurt and flabbergasted as I could ever remember. I resolved right then to make sure Dalton got a piece of my mind.

"From your description, I expected someone altogether more congenial," Cade said.

"I think he's just tired. He was up at the resort all night trying to catch some vandals in the act." I was making excuses for him. Why was I doing that?

"Right," Cade said also in a much more clipped tone than I was used to. It seemed the testosterone fairy had come and sprinkled a little too much of the magic dust around Gramby Estate.

Dalton's conversation with the coroner didn't take long. The cause of death was quite obvious, and there was little at the scene to help with the case. Cade had walked off to answer a phone call, which gave me a few seconds for a quick chat with Ranger Rude.

Dalton reached me and looked around as if I was hiding Cade somewhere in the garden.

"He walked off to take a call," I said before he could ask. "I'm sorry I told you you needed a nap. But jeez, did you have to get so grumpy about it?"

Dalton took off his hat and raked his fingers through his short, black hair before returning the hat to his head. "I'm sorry, Scottie. That's probably because I do need a nap. I was up at the resort all night. I thought I was going to have five or six hours this afternoon to sleep, but it's been one thing after another." He glanced back to the place where Saul lay limply over the patio table. "Now it looks like I've got a murder case. I knew Saul Bonelli. He was a character and a bit of a scam artist, but I can't imagine why anyone would kill him. I'm going to need to drive over and see his sister as soon as I'm done here. I have to say—" he added hesitantly, "I was surprised to see you here when I arrived." Was that the reason he'd been so snippy?

"Cade is a friend. We met yesterday."

He chuckled. "Sounds like quite a serious friendship."

"You definitely need that nap," I said sharply.

"Sorry again." Dalton looked across the garden. Cade was heading back toward us. "He seems stuck up. I hear he's some big author and the new owner of all this." He surveyed the overgrown garden and the old, weathered house sitting on its knoll. "Not sure why he'd want it."

"It has charm, and it's part of his family legacy. And Cade's not stuck up. You can hardly judge a person from a ten second introduction."

Dalton raised a brow at me. "Sounds like you've found a new friend."

"Nothing wrong with that." This time I was being curt, but I wasn't loving his tone. It was almost accusatory.

Cade reached us as my short comment fell through the air and smacked the ground between us. The instant tension between the two men was unexpected and more than a little unsettling.

"Mr. Rafferty, I'm going to need a statement from you."

"I have no problem with that. Did Scottie tell you about the hat?"

I'd been so shaken by the terrible friction between them, between everyone, I'd forgotten to mention an important detail.

"She didn't mention it." Again, Dalton was talking in a clipped tone.

"The green hat the victim is wearing was my hat. I'd left it on the table. He must have put it on when he sat down for his break. And since he was shot from behind—"

"Right. I've got your meaning. So you think you might have been the intended target?"

"I guess it's possible. I'm just not sure why or who."

"Ranger Braddock," the coroner's assistant called.

"Excuse me," Dalton said and headed that direction.

Cade and I were alone for a few seconds, standing in an awkward silence, the first since we'd met. He was the first to speak, and it was a doozy.

"You mentioned you were friends with the ranger, but I didn't realize you were *that* kind of friends."

My face shot toward him. "*What* kind of friends?"

"I mean in a relationship."

My laugh was probably a little too loud and spontaneous given the situation, but there was nothing I could do to erase it.

Cade pointed. "Ah there, see. That's definitely a laugh that says I touched a nerve. Since I've gotten nothing but an ice cold chill from the man since he arrived, I'm going to assume he thinks there's something more there too."

I crossed my arms.

"And there is the defensive arm cross," he added.

"I saved you a cinnamon roll and everything," I said.

"Oh, come on, you're not going to stand there and tell me there isn't something more than a casual friendship between you and the ranger."

"Dalton and I went to school together." Naturally, this was the time to leave out my very big crush on the guy. "We both recently moved back to Ripple Creek and, most importantly, he's engaged to the extremely beautiful, extremely wealthy owner of the Miramont Resort."

"Huh, could have fooled me."

"Why are we even discussing this? You might have noticed that you have a dead man hanging out on your patio, and I don't know why my voice is getting higher and more hysterical. I'm going to stop talking now. But you're way off on your assessment. There, now I'm really going to stop talking." I turned the invisible key on my lips.

"Fine, I guess I was wrong." Cade said in a way that assured me he considered himself anything but wrong.

I stuck to my vow of silence as Dalton returned to where we were standing.

"Mr. Rafferty, the coroner is going to remove the body now. I'm going to do a search of the area." Dalton sounded so official. Normally, I would have found it cute, but at that moment, it was irritating. He looked from statue to statue. "I got your message earlier about vandalism at the estate. Does it have to do with the missing heads on those statues?"

"Yes. Although, that problem seems trivial given the circumstances."

"Unless someone destroyed your statues and then came back to kill you," Dalton noted. "We need to have a talk." Dalton turned to me. "Scottie, if you don't mind—I'd like to talk to Mr. Rafferty alone."

"Actually, anything I have to say, I don't mind saying in front of Miss Ramone. She's been here with me from the start."

Dalton's jaw twitched. It seemed I was standing between two roosters, each one trying to fluff up its plumage a little more.

"It's not usually protocol," Dalton said tightly. "But I guess we can make an exception."

I was suddenly asking myself why I hadn't just stayed home to bake brownies.

nineteen

. . .

The tension between the two men had not eased much. I was really hoping it would, and now that tension was rubbing off on me. Mostly, I was annoyed with Dalton. He was supposed to be a professional, but for some reason he'd already formed a negative opinion of Cade.

Dalton pulled out a notebook. "If we go with the theory that you were the intended victim—"

"And it's just that," I interjected. "A theory. After all, Saul doesn't look anything like Cade from behind. He's shorter, squat and doesn't have the same shoulder span." As I listed Saul's description and made special note that his shoulders weren't wide, like Cade's, Dalton looked up from his notebook with an irritated brow raise. "Right, I'll just be a silent bystander, but everything I said is true."

"I'll write that down," he said begrudgingly. "Lack of an impressive shoulder span," he muttered sarcastically.

"Those were not my exact words but whatever." Both men were looking at me now. I tapped my lips to let them know I was finished with the commentary.

"Mr. Rafferty, can you think of anyone who might have a grudge against you?"

Besides you, Mr. Braddock, I thought wryly.

Cade was shaking his head before Dalton even finished asking the question. Then his face popped up. "Well... no, he wouldn't do anything like that."

"We're starting from ground zero. Any information will help us at this stage," Dalton said.

Cade adjusted his sunglasses. It seemed he was about to open up a touchy subject. "This place has been in a probate fight for years. The estate was left to my mother, but members of the family contested it. Unfortunately, she died just as the court awarded it to her. It passed to me, and I immediately found myself in another probate fight with my cousin, Jacob Gramby. He lives in California. The judge quickly ruled in my favor. Jacob was very angry. But he wouldn't resort to murder."

Dalton ignored the last comment and wrote down the name. "If you can get me his information—"

"No," Cade said a little too forcefully, then softened his stance. "I don't want to start a big family war."

"Mr. Rafferty, I'm going to need to cover all the angles."

"But what if I wasn't the intended victim? Like Scottie said —Saul and I don't look anything alike."

"If the killer came here with a plan, then the person they

were most likely to find on this property was you. How long has Saul been working here on the estate?"

"Just since yesterday," Cade said quietly. It seemed to be dawning on Cade that Dalton was right. This was his property. Why would the killer come looking for Saul on Cade's estate?

The mention of his cousin was interesting new information that Cade hadn't brought up before. I knew there was some sort of legal fight over the property. Rumors about the whole inheritance mess had been swirling around town for years. Could it be that a family feud over the property had pushed someone to murder? But why would it have taken someone so long to snap if the probate fight had been ongoing for years?

The coroner and his assistant had some trouble rolling the gurney topped with the filled black bag over the rough landscape. Their grim load bounced around on top as the gurney tires, not meant for rugged landscape, hopped and dipped along the way. My intuition was telling me that Saul was the intended victim. He could have told numerous people that he was working at the Gramby Estate. It would be a big deal for a small-time handyman like Saul. His brother-in-law certainly knew. If someone had a grudge against Saul, the remote estate would be the perfect place to commit murder. It was even possible the person didn't realize that the house was already occupied. Its ragged state still made it look abandoned.

I wandered away without any fanfare, only Dalton added

some of his own. "Where are you off to, Scottie? This whole garden area is technically a crime scene."

"I promise I won't disturb anything. I just want to have a look around."

"Don't touch anything," he added. I walked away feeling chastised and more than a little miffed.

I headed back in the direction of the wilderness where the shot probably came from. I was no expert on guns or ballistics, but as far as I knew guns always shot in a straight line. I glanced back at the patio. The hole in Saul's head was pretty well centered. Whoever shot him was highly skilled.

I walked out toward the untamed landscape and shuffled around in the brush and debris. Technically, I was not touching anything because I was wearing shoes. I'd climbed through some dense foliage, but this landscape had been untouched for years. A skittering in the nearby brush reminded me that rattlesnakes were still out and about. My shorts and sneakers were no protection from a pair of fangs. I stumbled back out of the landscape. If Ranger Braddock wanted to explore the area, he was welcome to it. I'd stick with the easier to traverse and less occupied by snakes areas, like the clearing around Saul's van.

The vehicle was parked in a spot that was mostly gravel. That made a hunt for evidence a little less daunting than the wilds of Ripple Creek. The two men were still talking. I was just as glad to leave their cone of tension. Their whole interaction with each other was baffling.

I'd already seen the contents in the front of the van, including the little love note wrapped around cookies. It was time to check out the surroundings. Maybe the killer left something behind that would spark a lead in the case. Look at me. I was even mentally talking like an investigator.

Considering how often trespassers and curious hikers had traipsed across the property in the last few years, there was little evidence of human existence. It was all nature, untamed and boundless. I stood at the highest point on the gravel parking area and swept my eyes around. The headless statues were the only things that stood out. It made sense. If the killer had come through the wilderness on a dirt bike, it would have been easy enough to climb off the bike, hike the rest of the way to the property, take the shot and then get back to the bike without leaving a drop of evidence behind. A highly-skilled hunter could have shot Saul from just about anywhere in the garden area without being seen.

I was about to give up my quest when a flash of yellow caught my eye. I'd been so interested in the interior of Saul's van, I'd somehow missed the yellow piece of paper crumpled up beneath it. In my defense, it was far enough under that I wouldn't have seen it standing so close to the van.

I peeked over at the men as I made my way across to the vehicle. Dalton was writing something in his notebook. I was sure it was Cade's account of where he was when the shot was fired and anything else he might have heard. Maybe Cade was giving him his cousin's information, after all. Family feud or not, it seemed like Jacob Gramby had motive. But who had motive to kill Saul, a middle-aged, unmarried small business owner?

I hated to do it, but I had no choice except to kneel on the gravel in order to reach the yellow piece of paper. Small rocks dug into my knees as I stretched my arm out as far as it would go. My fingertips just barely reached the paper. I couldn't get enough of it to grasp it. I took a deep breath, dug my knees deeper into the gravel and jolted forward. I managed to snatch a corner of the paper between my fingers. I pulled the paper free. After Dalton's admonition not to touch anything, I decided to sit on my bottom (what was a little more gravel, after all) and use the van as my shield from view.

I was no longer bothering with the napkin. I opened the crumpled paper. It was another handwritten note, only this one wasn't lovey dovey with sweet nicknames. Quite the opposite. The writing was messy, and it seemed the penholder had been angry while writing it. The message confirmed that.

"S—I NEED THAT MONEY OR ELSE. –K"

I'd talked to Kent Milner about his brother-in-law, Saul. There had been some kind of rift between them about money. I was sure Kent had written the note. I took a picture of the yellow paper, then carefully rolled it up to its original crumpled ball. I tossed it gently under the van. After the way Dalton had been acting, I decided he could find the note on his own. I was running my own investigation. I saw no reason to lend a helping hand to the official one. That reminded me, I still had the hardware store receipt in my pocket. I didn't want to get in trouble for taking possible evidence away from the scene, so I hiked over to the statue with the axe blade stuck in its neck and placed the receipt back in the grass. I'd already taken a picture of it. That was all I needed. It was getting late. I'd worn out my welcome on the Gramby Estate.

I planned to ride my bike into town for one more stop in my investigation before heading home. At some point during the hectic afternoon, I'd decided to make butterscotch cupcakes for the next farmer's market, and I needed to experiment with recipes. I'd found the murder investigation a nice little distraction from the thing pressing mostly on my mind —opening a new bakery.

twenty

. . .

The long days of summer were certainly coming to an end. It was only five o'clock, but it seemed as if the sun was already shrinking behind the taller peaks. The late afternoon air cooled my sun-kissed skin as I pedaled down Town Road. It was that sort of in between time of day when tourists and visitors had retreated back to their cars or rentals, and shops were cleaning up for the evening and getting ready for tomorrow.

Walt, the general manager of the sporting goods store, was a friend of Nana's. He was tall and thin and sort of boneless looking, like a scarecrow. White tufts of hair grew from the top of his head like a plucked chicken, and he had an infectious laugh. Nana and Walt were almost a couple at one point in time, only Nana just couldn't work up the romantic feelings needed to make the thing stick. He was always friendly and well-mannered to us even though Nana broke his heart.

I headed into the store. A few customers were trying on snow parkas. The winter gear had arrived, a downy filled reminder that the beautiful summer days would grow short and blustery. After an explosion of color in fall, winter would don its icy glower, and Ripple Creek would be filled with snow and nose numbing temperatures.

I was in luck. Walt, who, even at his age, insisted on doing a lot of the work in the shop, was hanging new snowboards on the back wall. He was about to lose his grip on one. I hurried to grab the end that was sliding down. He looked over, surprised. "Scottie! Perfect timing."

We secured the snowboard to the display hooks placed in the wall. He stepped back, admired his handiwork, then took a linen handkerchief out of his pocket to wipe his brow. "I know I'll regret saying this a few months into winter, but I'm getting tired of the summer heat."

"I agree you'll probably rethink that in the middle of January, but it works right now."

Walt headed back to the boxes of stock he was unpacking. "How is Evie?" he asked. "I haven't seen her in town much lately."

"She's fine. I think, like you, she's a little tired of the heat."

Walt dug a pair of neon pink snow boots out of the box and held them up. "I guess your friends can't lose sight of you on the slopes in these guys. What brings you in, Scottie? Can I interest you in some goggles?" He took out a pair of snowboarding goggles and pulled them down over his face. There was a sticker on the glass. Walt pointed to it. "I've asked them over and over again not to put a sticker on the lens, but they never listen." He pulled the goggles off.

"Walt, I was hoping you could help me out with something." As I pulled my phone out from my pocket, it occurred to me that it was not my place to talk about the murder. I could only assume word had not gotten around yet. I wasn't even sure if next of kin had been notified. However, news of the vandalized statues had probably already made its way around town. News didn't sit still for long in Ripple Creek. "You might have heard about the vandalism up at Gramby Estate." I scrolled through to the photo.

"I heard a few customers talking about it—something about old Arthur Gramby's statues getting destroyed. It was sort of coincidental because one of his descendants just happened to walk into the store yesterday afternoon."

I practically hopped up on my toes in interest. "Is that right?"

"His name was Jason or John or—" He tapped his chin in thought.

"Jacob?" I asked

"That's it. Jacob Gramby. I thought he might be the person moving into the Gramby home, only I'd heard another pair of customers, a couple of ladies, talking earlier in the day about how tall and elegant the new Gramby resident was. This poor man wasn't either of those things. He was sort of squarish in build with a scruffy looking goatee."

I was giddy about what I'd uncovered. I just needed to make sure that Jacob was in the store to buy an axe and not a pair of snow boots. I showed Walt the receipt I had on my phone. Walt stopped to pull out some wire framed reading glasses from his pocket. He took the time to wipe them with a small piece of soft cloth he'd had stuffed in the same pocket. I was like the kid waiting to be handed a cookie from the jar. My feet badly wanted to do a happy dance, like the ones football players performed after a touchdown.

Could it be I'd already solved the case? Had Jacob Gramby been so distraught about his cousin getting the estate that he plotted his murder? Maybe he'd vandalized the statues and then decided it wasn't enough. Maybe seeing his famous ancestor beheaded didn't give him the satisfaction he was craving. Then he spotted his cousin sitting out on the patio behind the mansion, sipping tea and enjoying his new life and he snapped. But where did he suddenly get a hunting rifle? He must have had it with him. He didn't live in Ripple Creek. Cade mentioned Jacob lived in California. He would have had to plan the murder before leaving home if he brought along a weapon.

Walt was like Nana. Whenever I showed her something on my phone, she made a big scene of putting on her reading glasses, then leaned so close to the screen her nose practically touched it. After squinting at the image for a few minutes, she ended up removing the glasses for a better look. Walt went through the exact same ritual. He pulled the glasses off and straightened.

"That's it. That's Gramby's receipt. He asked me for the strongest axe in the store. I led him to the Fisher Brand. You can cut a whole tree apart with one of those axes and barely break a sweat. That brand will last so long, you'll be handing it off to your kids and grandkids once you're too old to swing it."

Except if you're cutting off stone heads, I thought. The blade had gotten stuck in the stone, and the handle broke clear off.

"Did you ask him what he was using it for?" I asked.

"Sure, sure. He wasn't much for small talk, but since he wanted the strongest axe, I wondered if there was a tree or stump that needed chopping. He said a stump, but he gave it some thought before answering." It seemed to suddenly dawn on Walt what Gramby might have been doing with the axe. His bushy white brows did a little dance. "Hold on. You're not going to tell me that he used that nice Fisher axe to destroy those statues. It's a great axe, but it's not meant for stone. He should have been more specific." Walt smiled at his last comment. "I guess that would have been confessing to a crime, wouldn't it?"

"I think so. Still, you know your axes. That Fisher brand did not hold up to stone. The shiny new blade is stuck in one of the statues. The handle broke off."

"Gramby probably couldn't get it back out, so he broke it off on purpose so as not to leave any fingerprints behind."

I nodded, impressed. "You're right, Walt. I'll bet he did break it off, so he could take the handle and any evidence with him."

Walt rubbed the side of his temple. "What I don't under-stand is—how did you end up with the receipt?"

"Apparently, while he was busy trying to wrest the axe

handle free, he dropped another piece of evidence out of his pocket. I found it in the grass next to the statue with the blade."

"Well, I'll be. That's some good detective work, Scottie."

"Thanks. I've taken up enough of your time, Walt. Take care."

"I will and tell Evie hello for me. Remind her she promised to meet me for coffee."

I waved and walked out of the store. As I headed down the sidewalk, I spotted Esme locking up her shop. Her bookstore looked so inviting and attractive next to my dull brick building. I badly needed to get the remodel going. In its present state, the bakery was an eyesore, a blight in the middle of an otherwise charming town.

I crossed the street. "Hello, neighbor," I called.

Esme spun around. "Scottie, nice to see you. How is your day going?"

"It's been interesting, to say the least." I decided to let news of the death at Gramby Estate work its way naturally through town. Ripple Creek never kept a lid on significant events, and Saul's murder was definitely that. After meeting Esme, I realized how nice it would be to have a woman closer to my age to hang out with. If she was going to be my business neighbor, I hoped we'd become good friends.

"Listen, Esme, if you're not busy this evening, I'm going to be baking some treats to try out for next week's market. I can always use a taste tester. I understand if you can't make it."

Her face lit up. "I would love to be a taste tester. Thanks so much for asking me. I'm new to this town, and I'm embarrassed to admit, I'm a little short on a social life."

I was relieved and pleased that I'd asked her. "I'm not even new to this town, and I've got very little social life. I'm glad you can make it. Does seven work?"

"Perfect." She rolled in her lips. "I've been wanting to ask, but I didn't want to be too forward. Can we exchange phone numbers?"

I pulled out my phone. "Absolutely."

twenty-one

. . .

I found myself wanting to impress Esme. I'd ridden my bike home, happily, glad that I was going to have a new friend. It seemed silly at my age, but after cancelling my wedding, I'd realized that most of my friends were part of a group that had also been friends with John. Since I'd been the one to spoil everything, they all sided with him. The few friends I had to myself were disappointed in my decision, especially the part about moving back to Ripple Creek. I'd paid them back for their bridesmaid's dresses and even for the bachelorette party they'd thrown me, but they were still sore. I hadn't spoken to anyone since. It was probably for the best. I needed a clean break from life in the city.

"I smell brown sugar and butter," Nana said in a sing-song voice as she entered the kitchen. I'd warned her that since I'd spent so much time in town today I was going to need the kitchen for the rest of the afternoon. We ate some pieces of peanut butter toast for dinner, figuring that was all we'd need with the night of taste testing ahead of us. She was also pleased to learn that I'd invited the new bookseller, Esme, to try my butterscotch cupcakes.

I'd made the executive decision to test some new brownie recipes as well. It wouldn't hurt for me to show up with several items at the next market.

Nana stared into my bowl of whipping cream. Since the cupcakes were rich with brown sugar goodness and filled with a touch of caramel, I decided a whipped cream topping was the best way to counter the sweetness of the cupcake. "My mouth is watering," Nana said. It was another reason to have a second taste tester. My grandmother refused to ever find fault with anything I baked. She had been the same with my art as a kid, and I was no Van Gogh. I needed an unbiased opinion.

"When is your friend coming over?" Nana asked.

I lowered my frosting spatula and smiled at her. "That question just took me back thirty years. My *friend* should be here soon." As I said it, there was a knock on the door.

"Ah, there she is. I'll get it." Nana hurried to the front door. "Esme, so nice to meet you. The price of entry is a hug." She'd insisted on the same price when I was young. My friends never seemed to mind. They always preferred to hang out here, at Nana's house, than their own houses.

Esme carried in a bottle of white wine. She'd pulled on an orange sweater. It was the first time I'd seen her without her bookstore t-shirt. Her blue eyes were a sharp contrast to her black hair. She held up the bottle of wine. "My Grandmother

Sprinkles taught me never to arrive empty handed. I wasn't entirely sure what the proper gift was for cupcake tasting."

I took the bottle. "I think you made a good choice. We can pop it open after the treats." I turned to put the wine in the refrigerator.

Nana tilted her head in question. "Did you say Grandmother Sprinkles?"

Esme smiled. "That's what we called her due to the fact that she always made cupcakes with sprinkles."

"Is her real name Henrietta Parson?" Nana asked. The name sounded familiar as she said it.

"Yes, Grandma Etta, that's her," Esme said excitedly.

"She used to live in a small blue cottage at the other end of town," Nana added. "A group of us used to get together for a game of cards, and Etta always made her cupcakes with sprinkles. You're little Esme." Nana hugged her again. "The last time I saw you, you were in pigtails. How is Etta?"

"She's living in a retirement community near the city. And she's the belle of the ball. All the gentlemen are anxious to get a seat next to her on movie night."

"That sounds like Etta. How wonderful that you decided to move to Ripple Creek." Nana winked at me. "How wonderful that you both decided to drop anchor here. It's a wonderful place, and it'll only be made better by you two."

"I remember Henrietta," I said. "She used to bring those sprinkle coated cupcakes to the school bake sale. They were always the first to go. I just hope my butterscotch cupcakes can live up to them."

Esme and Nana sat down at the table. I put together a

sample plate with a cupcake and a brownie for each of them. The brownies had turned out perfectly, a crackly crust over a gooey center. (At least that was my idea of the perfect brownie.) Chopped, roasted hazelnuts helped break up some of the chocolate overload.

"All the town is buzzing," Esme said.

"Oh?" I asked surprised. It seemed news had already gotten around.

"Apparently, all the statues at the Gramby residence have been beheaded."

My shoulders sank. Only part of the news had gotten around, and it wasn't the most sensational part. "Yes, it's true."

Nana shot me a secret wink. I'd told her all about the murder. I'd also told her not to mention it until word got out. With the way Dalton had been acting, I was sure I'd get an earful if he found out I was spreading news of the murder around town.

I placed the treats in front of each tester with a glass of water for palate cleansing. It was a far less formal process than I was used to when I worked as a pastry chef in a high dollar restaurant. That was always a nerve-racking affair complete with investors and managers sitting in to give their opinions. I much preferred it this way, in Nana's cozy kitchen with friendly faces.

I sat across from them with my own samples.

"Who do you think would do such a thing?" Esme asked as she took a bite of cupcake. Her eyes turned up, and she moaned happily. "Hmm, this is so tasty." She took another bite and released another moan. "I just got the caramel surprise in the center."

Nana was taking smaller nibbles, making a show of being a proper taste tester. "Very good, Button. Sweet."

"Is it too sweet?" I asked.

"Not at all," Esme said, then shrugged shyly. "But then I have an enormous sweet tooth."

"I agree. It's not too sweet. It's delicious," Nana said. "And the cake is very fluffy and tender."

I took a bite too. "The sponge did turn out beautifully. I think this one will go on the cart next week."

We continued tasting and talking and laughing. It was a great way to end an otherwise chaotic day. I had my plans for the next farmer's market, and I'd been brainstorming some ideas for the interior of the bakery. Now, I had some new acquaintances and hopefully friends. Maybe my upside down life was finally starting to turn right side up.

twenty-two

. . .

I'd decided the best way for me to get inspiration for the bakery interior was to stand inside of it, even in its dreary state. The sellers had covered the windows with brown butcher paper making the place even gloomier. They'd said it was to keep curious thieves from looking in and finding something to steal. Not that there was anything worth risking a prison sentence for.

I leaned over the old work island. It was a warped sheet of stainless steel on four uneven legs. The whole thing wobbled side to side as I wrote down some ideas. After standing in the shadowy shop, I concluded easily that I was going to go with bright whites and pastels. Lots of built-in cabinets with glass doors to show off my treats and, at the same time, give the place that vintage feel I was hoping for. The front of the shop would be a confection for the eyes as well as the belly. Glass domes on ceramic glazed cake stands would display so many beautiful goodies, customers would have a hard time making a decision. The front of the shop needed a little corner nook with a few tables and chairs and plenty of room for long lines of customers (with any luck).

The few cabinets that remained were dingy and old and needed to go. I'd have to gut the place, but something told me once the old stuff was gone, I'd get a clearer vision of my future shop. I was looking forward to meeting with the contractor on Friday. I only hoped he'd be able to help me.

I was just about to step into the kitchen area, the area that was arguably the most important side to get exactly right, when a shadow passed across the paper covering the window in the door. It was still early, but people were starting to walk along the sidewalks. Only, this particular shadow stood, large and looming, in front of the door. After what happened yesterday, I was, admittedly, a little shaken. A knock startled me.

I walked to the door with my heart beating faster than it was supposed to. I peeled a bit of the paper back and was relieved to find Cade standing outside the bakery. He spotted me peering around the edge of the paper and waved lightly.

I opened the door.

"Hope you don't mind," he said. "I was taking a walk to the market, and I saw your bicycle." He glanced around. "Didn't know it was possible but this place is quite possibly sadder than the inside of my house."

"I agree. I'd offer you a refreshment to be polite, but all I have are some cobwebs and the food wrappers leftover from the wild raccoon party." I pointed out the empty chip bags on

Heads Will Cinnamon Roll

the floor. "Apparently, raccoons don't mind barbecue flavoring on their chips. How are you doing? Yesterday must have been stressful."

"I'm still kind of wondering if it was real or if I just woke up in one of my books. Ranger Braddock called to let me know it was officially a murder investigation but then I could have told him that without needing the shiny badge." There was still tension between the two men. "Saul was shot from about thirty yards. The person had good aim, or bad if he wasn't aiming for Saul."

"Well, I have a little bit of information that might shed some light at least from the perspective of the broken statues. You know that receipt I found from the sporting goods store? I paid a visit to Walt, the manager. He remembered the axe purchase, mostly because the customer—now prepare your-self, Mr. Rafferty—the customer was a Gramby. Jacob Gramby, to be exact."

Cade's face smoothed with shock. "You're kidding?"

"I wish I was." Before I could continue, Cade had his phone out.

"I'm going to call Jacob right now." I could hear the ringing through the speaker and then a voicemail recording.

Cade turned away but didn't move out of hearing distance. "All right, Jake. Very funny. I know you beheaded Arthur. You aren't a great vandal. You left the axe blade and a receipt behind. I'm keeping that receipt as evidence and so you can't get your money back. By the way, did you try and kill me too? Call me back." He hung up, seemingly satisfied that he'd left a perfectly reasonable message.

I, on the other hand, stared up at him unblinking and in a bit of shock.

Cade shrugged. "I'm a writer. I know how to get someone's attention." His phone rang. He pointed at it. "See what I mean?" He put it to his ear. "That was fast. So, did ya try and shoot me because if you did, I imagine you were a little surprised to see my name on the screen leaving a message."

His cousin spoke so loudly and nervously, from the tempo I heard coming through the phone, that I could hear his words clearly. Cade wasn't trying to cover up the conversation either. Maybe he figured since I'd solved the case of the statue beheadings, I was entitled to hear it.

"Look, yeah, all right, Cade. You caught me. I broke those heads off, and I can tell you it was satisfying taking that old guy's glower off those shoulders. He left the estate to the wrong side of the family."

"And your side of the family has been pouting about it ever since. Look, Jacob, I told you, if you wanted to come live here that would be fine. There are plenty of rooms."

"Why would I want to stay in that drafty old dungeon? I would have sold that place. That's what you should do. Then we can talk about sharing."

"I'm planning on living here, at least for now."

I mimicked a rifle being shot to remind him there was a far more important part to the phone call.

"Hey, Jake, so did ya try and kill me? Because I had a very dead handyman in my yard yesterday afternoon. He just happened to be wearing my hat so…"

There was a long pause. "Gee, Cade, I don't know

anything about a handyman. You mean someone died on the property? Mom always said that place was cursed. But it wasn't me, Cade. You've got to believe me."

"I want to believe you, Jake, but you did come on the property at some point to chop off Arthur's noggins."

"Yeah, yeah, I did that."

"I'm not going to press charges for it, Jake. I never liked those statues, but if there's anything else you'd like to confess."

It was one of the most entertaining and bewildering conversations I'd ever heard.

"Gosh, you know me, Cade. I walk around trails of ants so I don't kill 'em."

Cade pulled his phone away. "I've seen him do that," he mouthed to me.

"Besides, I'm already back home in California. I was there —you know—doing the damage—" Now his tone was more contrite than nervous. "I did that around two in the morning on Tuesday. Then I drove into Denver and took the 8 a.m. flight back to California. I've got a boarding pass to prove it. When did the handyman get knocked off? What happened to him?"

It was more than obvious that I had not already solved the murder case. I was disappointed, but after hearing Jacob through the phone, I was relieved he had nothing to do with it.

"He was shot in the back of the head around 1 p.m.," Cade said.

"Wow, what a way to go. Like I said, I was already back

home by then, and even though I used to be pretty good with a slingshot, I don't have the kind of aim to take a guy out from two states over." He chuckled. "But really, what a shame."

"Yep, well, I'll talk to you later, Jacob. Say hi to your mom and sisters. There's always room at the estate for anyone interested."

"Yeah, take care, Cade. And, uh, sorry about the whole statue thing."

"No big deal. Bye, Jake."

I was still flabbergasted by the conversation. From what Cade had told me, there'd been a long (I could only assume, expensive) court battle over the Gramby Estate. A case like that would have ripped family ties to shreds, yet Cade was talking to Jacob as if they frequently hung out together at social events.

"Think that covers that," Cade said. "Jacob was already back in California. He couldn't have shot Saul."

"I got that. I thought you might reach through the phone and give him a hug at the end. The man did fly all the way here just to vandalize your property."

"That was more of a cathartic experience for him. Arthur Gramby caused the rift between the two sides of the family, and Jacob let him know how he felt about it. I don't blame him."

"I need whatever kind of zen pills you take. But you know what? That's your business. If it wasn't Jacob, and, by the jovial little hugs and kisses to the family ending I just over-heard, we know that's the case, then is there anyone left who might want to kill you? You mentioned an ex-wife?" That question might have been more for my personal interest than the investigation, but I'd read somewhere that spouses, and especially ex-spouses, were always prime suspects.

"Katy lives in New York. Her new boyfriend is a pilot. I think we can check her off the list, especially because she left me for the pilot. If anyone was going to plot a murder it would be me. However, she is not worth life in prison, so you needn't worry about that plot coming to fruition. Useless chatter aside," Cade continued, "I honestly can't think of anyone out there who hates me enough to kill me. I don't have a lot of friends, but I also don't have a lot of enemies. I'm sort of a Switzerland of people. Like to keep mostly to myself."

I smiled at the analogy. "That's a good place to be. Not to get too personal—" I started.

"Oh go ahead. You know you're dying to." His cocky grin always deepened the lines on the side of his mouth that accentuated the smile.

I straightened and tugged the hem of my shirt for no particular reason except to look more serious. "Really. I want to get to the bottom of this. I've done it once before here in Ripple Creek, and I've discovered it's a rather satisfying pursuit—solving murders. That said—I just want to make sure we've covered all the bases for *Switzerland*." I looked pointedly at him. "Your ex is on the east coast, but what about dating? Surely a handsome, successful man like your-self isn't sitting home alone every Saturday night." Maybe I was straying a little more into just curious territory than actual investigative territory, but crazed people were everywhere.

Cade raised a dark eyebrow. "As long as you're not getting too personal. I tried a couple of those dating apps a few years back and decided, wholeheartedly, that they were not for me. If you're imagining some Glenn Close type from *Fatal Attraction* lurking in shadows waiting to eat my pet rabbit and shoot me dead, I think you're at another dead end."

"Right. Well, that was spoken with enough confidence that I think we can safely take obsessed lover off the table. I think that means we should consider the likelihood that Saul was the intended victim. While you were busy talking to the officials at the scene, I did some snooping around. I've got a few places to start."

"I have every faith in you," Cade said. "Although, I'm not exactly sure why. However, I did not get any warm, fuzzy, on the case feelings from the ranger."

"I don't know what was wrong with Dalton yesterday. He's not usually like that. I think he's just overworked. His fiancée has him hopping up the hill to the resort every time someone sneezes too loudly. I'm sure he'll figure out what happened... eventually..." I grinned. "After I figure it out. That's my goal. I better get out there on my trusty bicycle and get this case going." I walked him to the door. "I'm glad you stopped by. A lot of questions have been answered. What are you up to for the rest of the day?"

He stopped before walking out and lifted his hands to mimic them sitting over a keyboard. "My editor wants my chapters. While I don't think he'd stoop to shooting me in the head if I don't deliver, I have no doubt that he has at least daydreamed about that exact scenario more than once. I'm disappointed that I have to write. Solving a murder, especially when it's not my murder, sounds like way more fun. Keep me posted, Ramone."

"I will. And maybe avoid green hats. At least until I catch the culprit."

twenty-three

. . .

I'd locked up the bakery, leaving behind the dust, cobwebs and a stack of brainstorming notes. The whole thing was coming together beautifully in my head. Now, if I could just wiggle my nose and make it happen. I decided to head home and prepare myself a snack before venturing out on my quest for a killer. I was pedaling over the bridge when a vehicle rattled the planks beneath my tires. I glanced back over my shoulder. It was Dalton. He was waving at me to pull over.

I waited until I was clear of the bridge and pulled over to the side of the road. He passed me and parked his truck.

His tall, lean figure emerged smoothly and coolly out of the cab. "Excuse me, officer, was I pedaling too fast?" I teased. It actually put a smile on his face.

"I thought I saw smoke coming from those tires. Where are you off to at turbo speed?" I rested my bike down, and we leaned against his truck. The sun had warmed the metal enough that it felt nice against my skin.

"I'm going home to get a snack before I head out to—" I sealed my lips shut.

He waited. "Heading out to?" The hint of a glower appeared. "I'm not sure you should be hanging out with that guy, Rafferty, at his estate. As you might recall, there was a murder there yesterday. It seems as if he brought some trouble with him."

I was no longer relaxed enough to lean against his truck. I stood up straight. "He didn't bring trouble. In case you missed it, I already dumped my overbearing, bossy fiancé. I'm not looking for someone to replace him in the telling me how to live my life department. Or in any department, for that matter."

He'd stopped leaning too. "I'm just trying to make sure—" This time it was his turn to shut his mouth.

"Trying to make sure that you control my life? I don't think the killer was after Cade. I think whoever shot that gun knew it was Saul Bonelli sitting in that chair." We were both getting our feathers ruffled. I couldn't understand what had happened. We'd never spoken crossly to each other before.

"You do realize that you're not on this case, right? I know when Evie went missing, you dabbled in some investigation—"

"Dabbled?" A wind blew my hair, and a thick strand of it slapped me across the face. It wasn't the best way to start my rebuttal, and I had a hearty one at that. I pushed the hair away. "Do you mean when I *dabbled* myself right to the door of the killer?"

"I was on my way to arrest him, and you nearly got yourself killed in the process. That's why you need to stay out of this one, Scottie."

"And there he is again, trying to control my life."

He stepped closer, close enough that I could see every one of his long black lashes spiking up over his chocolate brown eyes. I had to admit, his nearness was throwing me off my defensive game. "I'm trying to make sure you don't get hurt or killed." His face came so close to mine, I could smell the soap on his skin.

I stared up at him. There was a long, silent moment between us where a flash of static electricity filled the air. I was sure I didn't imagine his long, heated gaze on my lips.

"So you care about me?" I asked, haltingly.

There was a long enough pause that I was sure he was coming to the same conclusion. His response was far from titillating. "It's my job to make sure everyone in town stays safe." It was like a cold slap, especially after the heated moment that I was sure had happened. Maybe it was just the sunlight reflecting off the truck.

"Well, thank you, Ranger Braddock. I'll sleep much easier knowing you're out here on patrol keeping all of us safe."

"No, Scottie, you know that's not how I meant it." He sighed and scrubbed his fingers through his short hair. "I'm just tired. Between the wedding plans and making sure the resort stays free of vandals, Crystal has me running a marathon every single day. Just stay clear of the investigation." A small smile broke out. "Besides, Evie would never forgive me if I let something happen to you."

I nodded. "Ah, I see. You're worried that your homemade waffle supply chain will be cut off."

He shrugged. "They're the best waffles I've ever eaten." I was relieved that the tone of our conversation had lightened. I didn't like the other side of Dalton I'd been seeing these past two days. While I had him, I figured it wouldn't hurt to grill him a little, find out what direction he was headed with the case.

"Do you have any suspects?"

He smiled but this time it was sort of an annoyed grin. "If I do, I'm certainly not going to start shouting their names about town. It usually works better when the suspects don't realize they're on the list. But since I'm seeing a little of the famous Scottie Ramone pout forming, I'll tell you that I'm focused on a family member, a cousin."

I held back a laugh. "You're still going with the assumption that the killer was after Cade."

"No assumptions. Who would want to kill Saul? He was a harmless guy who drove around in that ramshackle van trying to make a few bucks cleaning up gardens and tightening door hinges."

"Interesting. I will let you get back to your official stuff, and I'm going to go home and make myself a peanut butter and jelly sandwich on some of Nana's homemade soft white bread."

"Good idea. Remember what I said. Leave the murder cases to the professionals."

I saluted him as I strolled back to my bicycle. I climbed on the bike and glanced back. Surprisingly, he was still watching me, and darn, if I didn't see the tiniest glimmer of admiration in his dark eyes. Or maybe it was just the sunlight glinting off the truck again.

twenty-four

. . .

While I nibbled my delicious sandwich, I doodled out some of the things I already knew about the murder. It happened just after 1 p.m., and Cade was sure he heard the buzz of a dirt bike right before the gunshot. I knew of one teenager in town who constantly puttered around on an obnoxiously loud dirt bike. His name was Bucky, and he was around sixteen. Nana knew his grandmother, Eleanor, back in the days when Ripple Creek was mostly inhabited by struggling artists. Eleanor used to make pottery. I still had a clear memory of me sitting in front of her pottery wheel, giggling like crazy as I tried to get control of the cold, wet clay in my small hands. Nana still had the absolutely hideous ashtray I made sitting on a shelf with her other knickknacks. Eleanor had moved to Florida, but her daughter, Candy, still lived in town with her two children, Bucky and Janice. What if the whole terrible incident had just been teenage boys messing around with a hunting rifle? While the preciseness of the shot suggested otherwise, it was not unheard of for a stray bullet to find an unintended target. It was a long shot, but I'd start with Bucky. At the very least, if he had been racing around the trails on his bike that day, I could cross the dirt bike off the evidence list.

Candy and her kids lived close enough that it was an easy bike ride. The sky was a brilliant blue, and lush, mostly ever-green landscape made for a scenic ride. Candy's house looked a little more rundown than I remembered. Her husband, Ernie, had left a few years after Bucky was born. An attempt at a flower garden was now a patch of mostly weeds with a few tough zinnia blooms trying to stick it out. A skateboard, its plethora of stickers now faded, sat on its side just off the front steps. Two pots of hanging plants, mostly dead, swayed gently in the breeze wafting beneath the porch overhang. A tiny whirring hummingbird stopped at the glass feeder hanging next to the plants but to no avail. The feeder looked as if it hadn't been filled in weeks. Nana always panicked if her feeders were empty. She knew the birds counted on her vigilance, and she took her job very seriously. She would have been clucking her tongue at the sight of the empty feeder.

As I knocked on the door, I realized I wasn't exactly sure how I'd approach the subject. What if it had been Bucky and his friends messing around? They'd still be facing serious consequences. I hated to be the one to bring all this down on their heads. My worries were quickly washed away when an uneven thumping sound was followed by Bucky opening the front door on a crutch. His right foot was wearing a blue fiberglass cast. He didn't recognize me. There was no reason he should. I barely recognized him. I wouldn't have if I hadn't known I was standing in front of his house. He also had a noticeable white scar above his eyebrow, the one he got when he fell off the slide in the park, an incident that had made the local news.

"Hi, Bucky, I don't know if you remember me or not. My name is Scottie."

A long strand of bangs hung over his face. He flipped it back. "Yeah, I know you. My mom said you left some rich guy at the altar last month, so you could move back in with your grandmother. Not sure I'd make that choice but to each his own I guess." The bangs fell over his face again. This time he left them alone. Something told me he spent a good part of his day staring through those same strands of hair. "My mom's at work."

"Actually, I was hoping to catch you at home, and I see that I have." I stared down at the blue cast. "Did you fall off your dirt bike?" The broken foot pretty much ended this part of the investigation before it even got started. I was relieved Bucky had nothing to do with Saul's death.

"Nah, my bike hasn't worked all summer. Frame got bent when I jumped it off a slab of granite. I broke my foot riding my skateboard. What did you want to see me about?" It finally occurred to him how out of the ordinary this whole visit was.

"I'm friends with the new owner of Gramby Estate, and he heard a dirt bike out in the wilderness around his property."

This time he flipped the bangs clean off his face so he could make his case. "Wasn't me. I didn't break those statues. I heard they got their heads chopped off, but it wasn't me. Like I said, my bike is broken. I couldn't ride it even if it weren't."

"Clearly," I said once again looking at his cast. "Do you happen to know anyone else in town who rides a dirt bike?"

He shook his head. "Nope and I wouldn't snitch if I did know. My buddy, Gary, had to sell his bike. He's saving up for a car. I don't know anyone else who rides. Sorry. Can't help you." He glanced past me, apparently to make sure no one witnessed the conversation. I hadn't thought this through. Of course, a teenager was never going to tell on his friends or anyone else his age, for that matter.

"Thanks for talking to me. I promise I won't mention this conversation to anyone. Hope your foot heals soon."

The poor kid was so anxious to have me off the porch, the door snapped shut before my feet reached the bottom step. I wasn't exactly sure where to go next with my investigation. I knew for certain it hadn't been local boys messing around with a hunting rifle. I realized, as I climbed on my bike, that I was extremely relieved.

Before I came up with my next plan of action, I needed to make a pit stop at Roxi's store. She only had two boxes of brown sugar left the last time I was in, and I was going to need both of them for my butterscotch cupcakes. With any luck, a brilliant, new strategy would come to me while I pedaled toward town.

twenty-five

. . .

I realized halfway to town, my feet pumping the pedals and my heart rate moving at a good clip, that I'd missed riding my bicycle. It took me back to my youth when days were carefree and filled with thoughts of cute boys, sleepovers with friends and adventures with Nana. Admittedly, my legs were cramping up from being reintroduced to a bicycle, but the exercise was adding to my new found energy. I was angry with myself for wallowing in misery for the last month. I could have gotten so much done by now if I hadn't stayed in bed and on the couch all that time. But it wasn't going to help me to dwell on that unfortunate period. It just meant I needed to work twice as hard to make up for lost time.

Thanks to my taste testing panel, I had firmly decided to make butterscotch cupcakes and hazelnut brownies for the next farmer's market. Roxi's store was my main source for ingredients at this early stage of the game. The next nearest store was a long, winding trip down the mountain to the supermarket or an equally long and even more winding journey up the mountain to the exclusive and highly over-priced market near the resort. Apparently, if you could afford to stay at the Miramont, you could afford to pay fifteen dollars for a ham and cheese sandwich. As I scoffed at the notion of a fifteen dollar sandwich, I spotted none other than Crystal Miramont's black and gold Range Rover parked in the no parking zone in front of Roxi's store. It seemed even well-to-do Miss Miramont didn't like paying exorbitant prices for her groceries. And I supposed if your husband-to-be was the local ranger, then parking in a non-parking zone was not a problem.

I parked my bicycle at the bike racks. Crystal was just leaving the store with one small bag. It was a long trip for a few groceries. "Oh, Scottie, there you are. I was just asking Roxi, how come I never see Scottie in town?" Crystal's hair was blonder than ever, and her lips were as plump as two fluffy pillows. Her tiny tank top looked as if it had been purchased in the kid section, but she definitely didn't have a child's body. As I thought all of this, I was scolding myself for being so catty. But then, was it considered catty if all the comments stayed in my head? Either way, it wasn't good for me mentally to go so negative. I needed a fresh start with Crystal. She was going to marry Dalton, my longtime crush, and that was the end of it. No amount of mean-spirited thoughts was going to change that.

"Hello, Crystal, what brings you down the hill? A craving for one of Roxi's chicken salad sandwiches?"

"Gosh no, I'd never eat one of those mayonnaise drenched messes." She reached into the bag and pulled out a bottle of apple flavored kombucha. "They were all out up at Gaston's Market." Crystal looked past me to my bicycle. "How cute that you're riding a bike around town. I bought myself one of those new electronic bicycles. If I reach a big hill, I just push a little button and the bike practically glides up the hill. I don't even break a sweat. They're a little pricey though. You'll probably want to stick with the old-fashioned kind."

"The day I can't pedal a bicycle up a hill is the day I check myself into the retirement village." I'd tried to avoid a catty exchange, but Crystal made that too impossible. Every once in awhile, I wanted to blurt out that I had a bank account that probably bested her own, but Crystal wasn't worth it. I needed to get past my dislike of the woman and learn to live on the same side of the mountain with her.

She reached up to brush aside a hair that was not actually there. She was very transparent. It was her way of reminding me that she was wearing an enormous diamond (I'd sent mine back to John) and that she would soon be walking down the aisle to her new husband.

"How are the wedding plans going?" I asked, even though I had about as much interest in her wedding as I had in learning how book indexes were written.

She rolled her eyes right up into her lash extensions. "It's so much work putting on a wedding. I mean a proper wedding."

As far back as I could remember, Crystal Miramont had been the very definition of a snob. In first grade, she showed up with a Gucci backpack. At the time, I had no idea what that was, but our first grade teacher made her keep it in a locked cabinet with the teacher's purse because she didn't want anything to happen to it. The rest of us tossed our backpacks on hooks outside the classroom door. We once had to lock down the school because a black bear wandered onto campus. We all sat in our chairs watching in amusement and horror as the bear ripped open our backpacks to get to our granola bars and baggies of cheese puffs.

"I'm sure it's a lot of work."

She tapped me with her long fingers and extra long fingernails. "Oh, but I don't have to tell you. You were planning your own big, lavish wedding. I'm so sorry that didn't work out." There was nothing in her expression that said she was sorry. She looked pointedly at my ringless finger. The tan line was finally starting to fade. "It's a shame you had to give that beautiful ring back."

I lifted my hand. "That impractical thing? Couldn't be happier to be rid of it. And the man that came with it."

"Well, it's understandable if you didn't find the right match. I got so lucky with Dalton. We're perfectly suited together. Like we were made for each other."

I didn't see that at all but then I had a lopsided view of the whole thing due to my interminable crush on the groom. However, maybe it wasn't so interminable after all. The conversation with Crystal was definitely irritating, but I found that was mostly due to the fact that Crystal had irritating down to an art. My last few encounters with Dalton had left me with very mixed feelings about the man I'd always considered my soul mate. Maybe I was finally growing out of my Dalton Braddock stage. If so, it was about time.

"I suppose Dalton is equally excited about the big, lavish wedding," I said, knowing full well that wasn't true. "I would have taken him more as a simple ceremony in a mountain meadow type, but I guess I don't know him well."

"I guess not." She pushed a diamond tennis bracelet a little higher on her wrist. It slipped right back down. "Well, I've got a staff meeting. I need to head back up to the resort. It was nice seeing you," she said with nothing in her mannerisms or expression to back that up.

I returned an equally fake smile. "Yes, you too."

I hurried inside, happy to have that annoying chat out of the way. Apparently, Roxi had been watching through the window. She was wearing an amused grin. "Nice chat with Crystal?" she asked lightly.

I stopped in front of the counter. "If only I'd left my house five minutes later, but such is life and the tiny wrenches it likes to throw our way. Did you get my text about the brown sugar?"

Roxi leaned down and pulled two boxes of brown sugar out from under the counter. "My last two. I'm going to have to order more. You do realize when your bakery is open, you'll have to make special orders for ingredients?"

"Yes." I pulled out my debit card. "And I'm hoping my wonderful friend, Roxi, will be able to hook me up with a good wholesaler for things like flour and brown sugar."

Roxi put the brown sugar into a bag, so I could carry it on my handlebars. "I've got a few names that'll work. Seriously, when will we start to see some progress over there? Your building looks extra old and tired now that Esme has the bookshop remodeled."

"I agree. I've got a contractor coming to look at the place on Friday. In the meantime, I'm pulling together my ideas. I just hope the contractor will be able to fit my small shop into his schedule."

"Good luck with that." Roxi picked up a box of cookie packages and circled around the counter to put them on the shelf. "My friend, Andrea, up at the top of Starbrook, has been waiting for her bathroom to be remodeled for a year. The contractors are always so booked. Whenever she thinks they've finally found time to do the job, they cancel because something else has come up."

"That something being a much bigger more worth their time job. At least my bakery is a little bigger than a bathroom remodel. In fact, I need to do that too." I picked up the bag of sugar. "There's so much to think about still. I'm going to head home and search online for some good ideas. See you later, Roxi. Thanks for holding the sugar aside."

"Fortunately, there's not a huge rush on brown sugar in the middle of summer. Tell that grandmother of yours, she owes me a mocha latte and a long chat."

"I will." I stepped outside. The sun was starting to get lower in the sky, soon it would disappear behind the western peaks. I'd be glad to get home for the day. My legs were tired, and all the exercise had made me hungry. There was still so much planning to do for the bakery, I was almost overwhelmed thinking about it. My visions of new convection and proofing ovens were all muddled with thoughts about the murder. Who killed poor old Saul Bonelli? It might have been the unfortunate run in with Crystal or the sort of rude way Dalton had treated me, but more than ever, I wanted to be the first to find the killer.

twenty-six

. . .

The smell of grilled onions wafted from the kitchen out to the small nook Nana had carved out in the front room for her *office space*. When I was young, there was no computer in the house for years. Nana didn't think they had any use and that they only took up space. Then there was also some farfetched, unsubstantiated article about gamma rays or some kind of harmful rays rolling out of the monitors. I was in my first year of high school when I broke down into sloppy tears about how I had no way to research my term papers unless I sat in the library all evening. She finally decided to buy a used computer from a friend. It was slow and clunky and didn't have nice speakers like some of my school friends' computers, but I was able to cruise around the internet like everyone else. It didn't take too long for Nana to realize that the computer was a bonus and that if it was shooting out gamma rays, those rays hadn't made us grow horns or whatever else she was expecting to happen. It wasn't long before she was setting up her own artist's website. Now, I could safely say that as far as grannies went, mine was one of the most technologically savvy.

"Let's make a salad to go with these fancy grilled cheese sandwiches," Nana called from the kitchen.

I got up from the computer to help with the sandwiches. After looking at dozens of sites with bakery equipment, cabinetry and special cake and cookie stands, I was feeling overwhelmed. I needed so much, I didn't know where to start. Nana had suggested I work my way down, starting with the big stuff, the equipment that was essential to the running of the bakery, before picking out display cabinets and cake stands. The problem was that the latter was much more fun to buy than the equipment. I knew the brands I liked, ones I'd worked with in restaurant kitchens, but what I really needed was a contractor to do measurements and tell me what size everything should be.

"Ugh, so many decisions," I said as I entered the kitchen. The sandwiches smelled buttery and good. I plucked two ripe tomatoes and a cucumber out of the garden basket.

"There's a head of romaine in the crisper," Nana said. "I'm sure you'll get it all sorted. Starting a business is a big undertaking. Up until now you've only baked for other businesses. It's very different doing it all on your own."

"I'll say. I never gave it much thought because I always just used whatever was available in the kitchens I worked in. I want to make the right choices. Once the bakery is up and running, I can't very well switch out an oven or a refrigerator.

I have to make the right choices now." I washed the produce and began slicing tomatoes and cucumbers.

"You will," Nana said confidently.

"You're always like that, always positive, always insisting I'll do the right thing or make the right choice. But I was only a day and a half away from marrying the entirely wrong man. I'm not sure you should always trust me to make the right choices."

She turned to me, still holding her spatula. Our grilled onion and cheese sandwiches sizzled enticingly on a pan of butter behind her. "But you eventually made the right choice when it came to marrying John, so that one turned out just fine."

I decided cucumber chunks would work better in the salad. "I'm not sure if it turned out fine. I got out of a situation that wasn't going to work, and in doing so, I left quite the catastrophe in its wake. Even my friends aren't talking to me."

Nana waved the spatula. "Those are city friends. They're always fickle. Esme seemed pleasant enough, and you two will be neighboring shop owners."

"I'm looking forward to getting to know her. And then there's Cade Rafferty. He's fun to talk to. We sort of hit it off right off the bat." I put down the knife and turned her direction. "The strangest thing—Dalton showed up at the Gramby Estate to investigate the dead body. He and Cade met for the first time. I don't think I'm exaggerating when I say that hackles were raised almost instantly. For no apparent reason, the two men didn't seem to like each other."

Nana glanced back over her shoulder at me with a sly grin. "Is that so?"

I was mystified by her response. "Yes, that's so, and why do you look like the cat that's just caught the mouse?"

"No reason," she said and pretended to busy herself with the sandwiches.

"You're not going to tell me *no reason* when clearly your tone and expression say there's a reason. Out with it, Nana. What do you know that I don't?"

She played out the drama by carefully lifting the sandwiches from the pan as if they were fragile porcelain. Then she turned off the stove and set down her spatula. "Is the salad ready?"

"Almost and you haven't told me what you know. Wait. Is there something between Cade and Crystal? He acted as if he knew nothing about Dalton. Has he come here because of Crystal?" That notion made a lead ball form in my stomach. Was Crystal going to ruin that piece of my new social life too?

Nana rolled her eyes as she walked to the refrigerator for her homemade salad dressing. It was a delicious mix of balsamic vinegar, olive oil and fresh herbs from her garden. "I certainly haven't heard any rumors like that. Mr. Rafferty only just arrived, didn't he?"

"Then how do you already know that Dalton and Cade don't like each other?"

"I didn't know that. You just told me."

"Argh, you are such a tease." I unceremoniously dropped tomatoes and cucumbers into the salad bowls.

"It's just I think there might be a rivalry there because Dalton saw you with Mr. Rafferty and he got jealous."

A laugh shot from my mouth. "Jealous of what?" I shook my head. "Never mind. You're still dragging around that romantic fantasy about my thirteenth birthday wish finally coming true. I should have never told you that wish. You're never supposed to tell people what you wish for. That probably sealed the deal. Oh wait, that's not what did it. It's because Dalton never saw me as anything except awkward, slightly funny little Scottie Ramone. His opinion has probably not changed much since middle school."

Nana was keeping annoyingly quiet during my short protest. I placed the salads on the table next to the sandwiches.

"I think you might be wrong about the way Dalton feels about you."

"And I think you might be wrong about the way Dalton feels about me." I took a bite of sandwich and savored it. "But I forgive you for being wrong because you make a divine, melt-in-your-mouth grilled cheese."

"I certainly do." We both ate in silence a few minutes. It was so nice to be back in the kitchen I grew up in and sitting with the one person in the world who meant more to me than anyone. It might have been a few steps back in my adult life, but maybe that was all right. Maybe every adult should take a few steps back every once in awhile to connect to the things they love and miss the most about growing up. I certainly missed Nana's grilled cheese.

"What has happened with the death of Mr. Bonelli?" Nana asked. "I still haven't told anyone."

"It hasn't reached town yet, either."

"That's probably because the estate is off on its own remote hill. No one pays too much attention to that side of the bridge. I'm sure by tomorrow it'll be talked about in every corner of the town. Does Dalton have any idea who killed him?"

"If he does, he's not going to discuss it with me. He basically told me to keep out of it. It was phrased differently, but that was the gist."

Nana peered at me over the sandwich in her hand. "And are you staying out of it?"

"I was first at the scene. I feel a certain duty to see this one through. I'm just not sure where to start."

"How about Mr. Bonelli's enemies?" Nana asked.

"Yes, how about them," I said to myself. "I've been focused on Cade's enemies, but now, it's time to turn that page and move on."

Nana's eyes widened. "Mr. Rafferty's enemies? Why is that?"

"Saul was wearing Cade's green hat. He was sitting on the patio chair when he was shot. It seemed the killer only saw him from behind."

Nana nodded. "Ah, a case of mistaken identity."

"That was the first theory to emerge, but I think all that did was throw us off the track of the real killer. I think someone came up to the Gramby Estate to kill Saul Bonelli."

"Maybe he had a disgruntled customer," Nana suggested. "You should look on that Whelp site and read his reviews."

I smiled. "Do you mean Yelp? You know what, that's a good idea. I wish I'd thought of that. I'll start that research as soon as I'm done eating this yummy sandwich." I had my next steps… thanks to Nana.

twenty-seven

· · ·

A crystal clear night gave way to an endless carpet of glittering stars. The moon sat like a gold crescent floating in a sea of diamonds. Nana was an avid stargazer. I carried my laptop out and joined her on the wooden picnic bench in the backyard. A comforting quiet surrounded us as we sat with cups of hot tea, our legs outstretched as we rested our backs against the table and stared up at the vast universe.

"It always amazes me to see nights like this," Nana said. "It's hard to fathom how endless this sky actually is. It's one of those concepts that's impossible to get your mind around. How can something go on forever?" She glanced over at me. "I'm so glad to see you up and about, Button. I won't lie. I was getting worried."

I sighed wearily. "I was too. I kept questioning whether or not I did the right thing. I devoted a number of years to John.

It felt as if all that time had been wasted, and I'd just tossed a chunk of my life away."

She patted my leg. "You'll make up for lost time, and soon the town will have a wonderful bakery. People will be lined up around the block to buy your goodies."

"That would be nice. I just wish it were already up and running."

"What about those reviews? Are you sure it's Yelp and not Whelp?" Nana asked.

"Just like I'm sure there's never been a Neverland Hall in an Austen novel." I opened the laptop and looked up Saul Fixes All on Yelp. It seemed his brother-in-law was not far off on his critique of Saul's business practices. His average rating was two stars. There were a few four-star reviews from people who were satisfied with a yard cleanup or a disposal replacement, but the most consistent comment was about Saul being lazy, taking long breaks and not finishing the work. A one-star review caught my attention because it was in all caps, and it started out with a big warning "DO NOT HIRE."

Nana had been gazing up at the stars. She straightened to refocus on my computer screen. "Anything worthwhile?"

"Here's one from a woman named Dana Forrest. She actually put her name, which helps make it more legitimate than someone named *anonymous*. Sounds like she has every reason to be extremely angry with Saul."

"Dana Forrest," Nana said. "I know her."

"Of course you do. Tell me, Nana, is there anyone on this

whole mountain who you have not at some time or another been acquainted with?"

Nana shrugged and pulled her knitted shawl tighter around her shoulders. "When you've lived for a hundred years—"

"You are not a hundred years old," I reminded her.

"No? It sure feels like I am. I feel like I've already lived enough for five lifetimes, which is why I know so many people. Dana Forrest bought a few pieces of my artwork. She's about twenty years younger than me. Last I heard, she lost her husband, Roland. He died of a heart condition. I haven't spoken to her for years. She lives a few miles south of here in a sweet little ranch house. What does she have to say about Saul?"

I clicked open the review and read it aloud. "Saul Bonelli is a flim-flam man. He'll take your money and make many promises, but he won't deliver on any of them. Saul told me he could remodel my entire kitchen for ten thousand dollars." I glanced up at Nana. "That should have been her first clue. Ten grand barely gets you a new bathroom these days." I returned to the review. "I gave Mr. Bonelli a five thousand dollar deposit. He came in and gutted my current kitchen then disappeared. He left me with wall studs, hanging wires and jutting pipes. I had no kitchen. He wouldn't return my calls. He is not to be trusted. Stay far away from Saul Bonelli."

I rested back against the table. "What do you think? Is Dana Forrest a killer?"

"I only knew her briefly so I couldn't tell you that, but I think if I handed someone five thousand dollars and they came in and destroyed my kitchen then disappeared, I'd be thinking about murder."

"I don't know. Whoever killed Saul knew how to shoot."

Nana looked at me with disappointment. "Is there any reason a woman couldn't have made that shot?" Nana was one of the original feminists. She'd seen a lot of progress in the past seven decades. She never liked it when someone said something that put women back a notch. Like my comment.

"I was thinking more about her age, but you're right, my mind went straight to a male when it was made obvious that the killer had terrific aim. You said Dana was about twenty years younger than you, so I'm picturing a woman in her sixties."

An arched brow met my comment.

"You're right. Now I'm saying that older people can't have skills like being able to shoot someone in the head from many yards away. I'll go see her. Just not sure how to approach the murder."

Nana laughed. "Be blunt. It's always worked for me."

"That's because you've mastered the skill of not beating around the bush. People expect it from you. They respect you for it."

Nana's head tilted side to side. "Some people dislike me for it."

"True but mostly it's respect. I have no such reputation. I'll have to ease my way into it."

Again, Nana chuckled. "Of course, I didn't mean you should march up to her door, knock and then blurt out 'why did you shoot Saul Bonelli?'"

"I wasn't planning on that." My phone beeped in the house. I groaned. "I'll bet that's another bill from Mrs. Rathbone."

"Speaking of bullets, I'm glad you dodged that one. Can you imagine that woman as your mother-in-law?"

The question sent an actual shiver through me as I opened the back door and went inside. I was more than pleased to see it was a text from Cade. Our first communication since exchanging numbers.

"Hey Ramone, I'm sending out the maiden voyage text. What about that sky tonight, eh?"

"I'm a little disappointed I didn't get to send out the maiden voyage text. The sky is fabulous. Nana and I have been sitting outside stargazing." I was still stunned at how instantly we'd become familiar with each other, as if we'd known each other forever.

"That's what I've been doing. It's a little creepy knowing I'm sitting at the same table where someone died. Your ranger friend is coming up to see me in the morning. Do you think he's onto something?"

"First of all, you can just call him Ranger Braddock rather than always adding in the qualifier 'your friend'. And I am not privy to his investigation, so I have no idea."

"You know a text conversation has gone south when the word privy is being tossed about. This requires a topic change. I think you should bake brownies for the next market. I miss my grandmother's gooey brownies."

"You must have been reading my mind. I am baking brownies for the market."

"Great. I'm just sorry the market isn't until next week. I'll let you go, Ramone. My regards to the stars above."

"Night, Rafferty."

Nana stepped inside. "What has you smiling like that?" she asked.

I reached up and touched my face. "Am I smiling? I didn't notice." I glanced at the text exchange before setting down the phone. "Nana, I'm going to bake some brownies. But don't worry, I'll clean up after myself."

"Brownies? At this hour? May I ask who they're for, or do they have to do with that big smile you were wearing?"

I smiled again. "Might have something to do with that."

twenty-eight

. . .

N ana had some brown parchment paper and cooking twine. I wrapped the cooled brownies like a gift package and even added a twine bow on top. Nana was finishing her cup of coffee on the front porch when I stepped outside.

"We might get a thunderstorm later," Nana said.

The first sign of possible storm clouds was visible in the distance. If a good breeze kicked up later this morning, it would push the clouds down into the valleys below, leaving behind only blue skies. I was hoping that would be the case, even though a little precipitation would be welcome. My plans, at least for this morning, were for a bicycle ride to the Gramby Estate. Nana had pulled the white basket she used to use on her bike down from the garage shelf. It looked truly dorky on my bicycle, but it would come in handy. Besides, wasn't I already past the age of looking dorky? It seemed a certain amount of dorkiness was expected once a person crossed the threshold of forty.

I placed the brownies carefully in the basket and climbed aboard. Admittedly, neither my bottom nor my legs had relished the idea of another day of bicycling, but the brisk ride and exercise had helped my spirits so much, I was willing to put up with sore muscles. I was sure the soreness would eventually be replaced by newfound strength and energy and, with any luck, some muscles in my legs.

I left Rainbow Road and headed toward the bridge. Dust up ahead signaled that a vehicle was coming from the opposite direction. A clearing of that same dust let me know that I was about to have another run in with the local ranger. My basket shifted side to side as I lifted my hand long enough to wave. I hoped that would be all that was required between us before we both headed our own ways. I remembered now that Cade had mentioned the ranger would be paying him a visit this morning. It seemed my timing was almost perfect. At least I'd missed Dalton's visit to the estate. However, it seemed my wave wasn't going to be enough. He pulled the truck to the side of the road and climbed out.

"Not another speeding ticket, officer," I teased.

"No, I'm pulling you over for excessive cuteness. I haven't seen a basket on a bicycle in a long time." He leaned down. "Do I smell brownies?"

There wasn't going to be any way out of this one. "Yes, you do."

He continued to stare into the basket. "They look as if they've been wrapped up like a gift."

"I guess that's one way to look at it, or maybe, I just wanted to make sure they didn't get dusty when I raced through town on my two wheels."

Dalton glanced back toward the bridge. "Are you taking them to Rafferty?"

"Is that an official question? Because, if not, it sounds sort of personal."

Dalton shrugged. "Just be careful, is all I'm saying."

I was on defense again. I wasn't loving this new thing between us. "Sounds to me like you're saying 'don't take brownies to Cade Rafferty'."

"It's not that," he insisted and straightened his posture. "In case you forgot, I'm investigating a murder, and the man you're delivering brownies to was most likely supposed to be dead instead of Saul Bonelli. He's new to town. What do you know about him anyhow, Scottie? He might be caught up in something shady. That's usually how people end up dead."

"Sounds like a lot of conjecture if you ask me."

His face didn't get red, but he did stick a finger under his uniform collar to loosen its hold on his neck. "The man's property was vandalized hours before his handyman was shot dead. And that handyman was sitting at Cade's table and wearing his hat."

"I was there, remember?" I stared at him, shocked at how unusually calm I felt. Normally, all it took was an accidental meeting with Dalton to send my pulse up to warp speed. We were facing off in what felt almost like an argument, and I was as cool as the proverbial cucumber. Had I finally outgrown my ridiculous crush on Dalton or was it only because I knew he was officially off the market? Maybe it was just good old self-preservation kicking in, or maybe Ripple Creek's newest resident had enough edge and good looks to dim my view of Dalton.

"Yes, I remember, and it seems you're going there again. The estate is the scene of a murder investigation."

"Once again, I was there. Is this about the brownies? I can make you some too." I added a smug grin.

"It's not about the brownies," he said emphatically and then paused. "Although, they do smell really good." A smile followed.

"They're gooey and rich, and they have chopped hazelnuts. I could give Crystal the recipe. I'm sure she'd love to bake you up a batch."

His eyes rolled ever so slightly. "Crystal isn't exactly the brownie baking type. She doesn't like to have sweets in the kitchen because she avoids eating anything with sugar."

"Well, it's good to know she has to make sacrifices to keep that figure. By the way, about the case…" I put up my hand. "Before you start a boring lecture about me keeping out of it, I just wanted to say that my intuition tells me the killer knew exactly who was sitting at that table in the green hat. Saul was short and stout. The complete opposite of Cade." I added a little salt on the wound. "Cade and I spoke at length about his possible enemies." The earlier comment about Cade's physique wasn't nearly as *salty* as my last sentence.

"Then you have been nosing around this case." His faint smile was gone again. "I thought as much."

"Cade and I are becoming fast friends. We talk."

"Clearly. You even bring him brownies."

"Really? You're still not off the brownie thing? I'll just lay it all out there then. Last night, Cade and I had a nice text conversation, and he mentioned he would really like to taste my brownies. One might even say our texts were flirty." I added that in even though I had no verifiable proof of it. Cade had this way of conversing that always bordered on flirty. And I liked it.

Dalton's jaw looked tighter than usual. (He did have an incredible jaw, clenched or not.) Was Nana right? Was I the reason for the instant rivalry between the two men? I had to internalize a loud laugh. Two men fighting over Scottie Ramone was as farfetched and comical as a cow literally jumping over the moon.

"I've wasted enough time with this conversation," Dalton said coldly.

"Uh, you're the one who stopped. I waved, which is the polite way of saying 'hello, but let's not talk' to someone."

"Sorry I stopped then. Thought I'd say hi to my friend, but clearly, you would have preferred me to drive on."

I'd pushed one button too many. "No, Dalton, really. That's not what I meant." Then I did something without thought. I grabbed his wrist before he turned away. He stared down at my fingers wrapped around his arm. I wasn't imagining the surge of heat where our skin touched.

"I don't like this between us," I said quietly. "I consider you one of my good friends, and I don't want to lose that." I released my hold on his wrist.

He didn't lift his eyes to meet mine. "Same here, Scottie.

Sorry about all that." His dark eyes met mine. Our gazes locked for a few seconds. It wasn't a normal kind of lock. It was filled with magnetic energy. I temporarily got lost in it all.

"Just be careful, all right?" he said.

"I'm a big girl. I'll be fine." That was the end of the conversation. Dalton walked back to his truck, and I climbed on my bicycle. Before my feet landed on the pedals I glanced back over my shoulder. I could see his face in the rearview mirror. He was watching me. Just like I was watching him. Somehow, in the midst of everything, Dalton and I had managed to tangle up a perfectly easy and solid friendship.

twenty-nine

. . .

Something about the whole conversation with Dalton had given me a shot of adrenaline. While he chased down Cade's invisible enemies, I was going to take a different path and search out Saul's enemies. Once the gravel on the drive up to the estate got too loose for my bike, I parked it and climbed off. I grabbed the parcel of brownies and hiked toward the house.

Cade was sitting outside on his patio wearing a white shirt and definitely not wearing a green hat. He was staring at his laptop, but his fingers weren't moving over the keyboard. He looked up when he heard me crunching through some of the garden debris.

He had a blazing white smile. "Ramone, what a nice surprise. I'm sitting here in front of my computer, but nothing is coming out of these fingertips." He lifted his hands to emphasize the fingertip point. His hands were long and suntanned.

I placed the package on the table. "Brownies. An early sample."

"You are my new best friend," he said as he pulled the package toward him. "But don't let that get to your head because my actual friend list is limited."

"Then I *will* let it go to my head because that means I'm on a very exclusive list, and now, according to you, I'm at the top of that list."

"Well, I still have to taste the brownies." He motioned toward an empty chair. "Have a seat at my murder table."

I pulled out a chair and sat down.

"See, that's what I like about you, Ramone. You don't let a little thing like the phrase murder table stop you." He glanced at the table. It was planks of a hard wood, maybe teak, put together on a rectangular frame. "I really like this table, but I'm thinking of replacing it, you know, because of the whole dead guy draped over it issue."

"I'd give it some time. The shock from that might wear off soon. After all, people buy houses where people died all the time."

"That's true. Arthur Gramby died right up there on the top floor, while sitting on his chamber pot, or so the story goes. Toppled over to the side and took the whole thing with him."

I laughed. "You're making that up," I insisted.

He held up three fingers. "Scouts honor. That is what I've been told. Although, it's possible the serving staff came up with the humiliating death as a final act of revenge on a master, who, by all accounts, was mean and miserly to work for."

"Then good for the household staff."

Cade untied the twine and unwrapped the brownies. "This was incredible of you, Ramone. I really needed this chocolatey pick-me-up." He took a bite, chewed and swallowed. "Your new best friend title has been solidified."

"Good to know. I ran into Dalt—Ranger Braddock at the bridge. What did he have to say? Is he any further on the case?"

He was shaking his head as he finished the brownie. "I don't think he's any further than when he first stepped onto the property with his copper attitude."

I chuckled. "Copper? Someone's been watching Victorian murder mysteries."

"Guilty as charged. I find that era helps me with the gothic tone in my novels. Something about dark, dirty London streets, gas lamps flickering in the fog and Ripper like characters skulking around corners gives me just the spark I need to create my fictional world."

"Hmm, I'm going to have to pick up one of Cade Rafferty's novels. And I do apologize for not already having read one, but for the last four years, I've been locked in a suffocating relationship with an overbearing man who admired his own reflection in the mirror far more than he admired me."

"Ouch. That ex just got filleted, salted and hung out to dry."

"I suppose so, but you know what—it felt good to get that off my chest. Thanks for listening."

Cade winked. "What else are besties for? And back to the *ranger*," he said it with enough derision to assure me their meeting this morning had not gone any better than the previous ones. Nana's suggestion of a rivalry all due to little old me popped into my head for all of a second before my voice of reason stepped in to quash it. "The ranger is still pursuing my enemies. He's convinced that Saul was not the target. In his words, and I quote—" he paused. "Well, it's not really a quote because I find myself drifting off mentally when Braddock speaks, but I think he said he couldn't think of any motive a person would have to kill a local handyman. When I told him I'd overheard Saul, on the morning before his murder, on a contentious phone call that seemed to have to do with money, Braddock jotted it down, but I think he was doing it for show. I doubt he'll look into it."

"Actually, I think I heard that phone call, only I was listening to the other end. Saul's brother-in-law, Kent Milner, happened to be standing in front of my cart at the street market when he was on his phone. He had an angry exchange, definitely about some money owed. That was when Kent told me that Saul was a terrible handyman. Kent did not have much respect for his brother-in-law, but the question is—did he dislike him enough to kill him?"

"Money issues can drive people to do desperate things."

I nodded. "Kent gave me his business card. He's a successful realtor. I doubt he was scratching the dust for money. It must have been a significant amount. Maybe Kent lent Saul money, and he never got paid back. I found a crumpled note beneath Saul's van the day of the murder. It was brief and threatening, about needing the money or else. It was signed K. It doesn't take a detective to figure out that the note was from Kent."

"And that is why you never lend family members money. Braddock mentioned something about relatives who had a problem with me. I told him all about the probate fight but that I was sure most of that side of the family had come to terms with it all. I decided to let him know that Jacob had caused the damage on the property but that I wasn't pressing charges. I also told Braddock that I talked to Jacob, and he had a solid alibi. He was in California at the time of the murder. He was going to double check the alibi. I texted Jake to warn him. Braddock was pretty disillusioned with my enemy list. He asked if that was all as if I was holding names back, but honestly, who would do that if they thought they were a target for murder. Which brings me to this—I'm convinced the killer got his prey. Someone wanted Saul dead, not me. I said as much to Braddock, but he seems determined to make me the rabbit in this case."

"I agree with you. While the ranger is out looking for motive to kill Cade Rafferty, I'm going to look for motive to kill Saul Bonelli. Was it money? Did he leave a customer wholly unsatisfied? Dana Forrest," I muttered.

Cade raised a brow in question.

"Dana Forrest wrote a bad review about Saul on Yelp. Allegedly, he absconded with a five thousand dollar deposit and left the poor woman with a gutted kitchen."

Cade looked approvingly at me. "You've been doing your research, Inspector Ramone."

"Can't take the credit. It was my grandmother's suggestion. However, she wanted me to look at the Whelp site."

Cade chuckled. "Is that the site where puppy owners write good and bad reviews about their puppies?"

"Wouldn't that be fun? Only, those poor puppies. I can't imagine there'd be many five stars. They might all be cute and fuzzy, but I've never met a pup who wasn't a total rascal."

"Ramone, I think in our spare time we need to create that Whelp site. Deal?"

I nodded. "Deal. Well, I don't want to take up any more of your writing time, and I've got a motive to chase down."

"I'm jealous again. I'm chained to my laptop. I've got to get some chapters over to my editor. Otherwise, I really might be the next body draped over this table. Although, Mitchell is more a poison in the wine glass type. I doubt he's ever held a gun."

I stood up. My legs were feeling all the bike riding, but it was a good, rewarding kind of ache. "I'll let you know if I make any progress."

"Please do, and I hope your progress is better than mine."

thirty

. . .

N ana had given me directions to Dana's house. I had to
ditch the bike and basket for four wheels. The ride
down to Dana's would have been a breeze on the bike. The
return trip, not so much. A white work truck, complete with
toolbox and ladders in the bed, was parked in the short brick
driveway. The house was a seventies brick ranch with small
windows and a semi-flat roof. The oak front door was
propped open by a wedge of wood, and the explosive sound
of a nail gun blasted through the open doorway every few
seconds. A worker in off-white coveralls and a pair of safety
ear muffs was running a long piece of wood through a table
saw. It seemed Dana had managed to finally get her kitchen
going.

I never knew the protocol when a door was already open
and not really available for a solid knock. I called into the
house, but the construction noise drowned out my voice.

Then, I got lucky. A sixty-plus woman with wispy pinkish-blonde hair, high cheekbones and neatly drawn eyebrows crossed from the hallway toward the noise.

"Dana!" I blurted before she got lost in the chaos.

Her face snapped toward the doorway. "Yes?" she asked. The neatly drawn brows stayed almost perfect as she pinched them together. "Are you with the crew?"

I hadn't been invited in, but I took a step into the entry. "Actually, no, I'm Scottie Ramone, Evie's granddaughter." Tossing my grandmother's name around was my usual calling card. Once again, it worked.

"Oh my, Scottie. Evie always talked about you. How is dear Evie? I've been meaning to stop by and see her. I'm going to need a few paintings for my new kitchen."

"I'm sure she could paint you something special. I see there's a lot of work happening. That was what I came to see you about." I startled. The nail gun had fallen into a rhythm where you knew when to expect the next bang, but it still didn't soften the impact.

She clapped her hands together softly. "You need a good contractor. Bill has been amazing. I'll get you his card."

"Well, no—actually, yes, that would be great." For a moment, I forgot my primary job was baker and not murder investigator.

"Please, come into the front room where it's not so noisy. I'll get a business card for you. I got lucky and found Bill's advertisement in the local paper. My first contractor turned out to be anything but professional."

"Or a contractor," I muttered, but she'd already gone off to fetch the card. The worker who'd been sawing wood carried the pieces through the entry and into the work area. It did seem that Bill's crew had their act together. If Dalton's friend didn't work out, I had a second number to call. It seemed kitchens were on their list.

Dana returned with a business card. I glanced at it and stuck it in my pocket. I was so new at this investigative thing, I wasn't exactly sure how to start. I took the Nana style path of straightforwardness. "Dana, I don't know if you know this, but Saul Bonelli was killed earlier this week."

Her chin dropped, and it looked genuine. "You're kidding. What happened? Did he fall off a roof? I don't think he ever took safety precautions. He demolished my entire kitchen without so much as a mask or pair of goggles. That should have been my first clue that he had no idea what he was doing. I was trying to save money, and he gave me such a low quote." She took a deep breath. "I've learned my lesson now. If you cut corners, you eventually pay the price. How did you say he died?"

"I didn't, actually." The nail gun stopped. It left behind echoes that seemed to just be in my ears. I was glad my remodel wasn't going to take place where I lived. "Saul was shot."

Her hand flew to her mouth. "He finally pushed it too far with his flim-flammery. I know I wasn't the only one who lost money to Saul Bonelli."

"Yes, I saw your review on Yelp. It was surrounded by a lot of other bad reviews." As I said it I realized how hard it would be to find the killer based on negative reviews. One thing was clear, I wasn't looking at a killer. I glanced around her front room. The walls were covered in paisley wallpaper, and some of Nana's artwork was displayed. There was no rifle rack or mounted deer head, nothing to indicate that sweet little Dana owned or knew how to shoot a hunting rifle. Fortunately, Dana didn't seem to put together my real reason for a visit. I moved on hoping she had some more insight into the man himself.

"Other than his questionable business practices, do you happen to know anything else about Saul? Anything that could help find his killer?"

Her mouth pursed in confusion. "Are you with the police?"

"No, but Saul died on my friend's property. I've taken an interest in his murder."

Dana shrank down and scooted closer. She was wearing some kind of powdery lavender perfume that made my nose tickle. It was a small price to pay if she had something noteworthy, and the hunched shoulders and expression on her face indicated she did.

"I got the impression that Saul considered himself quite the ladies' man. The few days he was here, he kept taking calls from someone he referred to as Bunny. I knew he was talking to a woman because his voice would drop lower. He'd talk smoothly and add in lots of words like honey pie and sweetums. I asked him once if he had a girlfriend. He laughed, told me he had a little black book as thick as an encyclopedia. I figured he was exaggerating. That should have been my cue not to believe a word he said."

I was confused. "Do you think he was pretending to talk to a woman?"

"Oh no, those calls were quite real. She rang him most of the time. Once or twice, he had to comfort her because something had upset her. The most interesting thing I overheard —" Dana paused. "Not that I was eavesdropping, but as you can see this house is small. I was usually sitting right here on my couch, working on my knitting." She pointed out the basket of yarn topped off with two knitting needles. "Saul would be in the kitchen. His voice carried right out here to the living room. Hers too. I couldn't usually make out her words, but I could hear it in her tone when she was upset. Happened more than once."

"Do you have any idea what she was upset about?"

Dana inched closer yet again. She seemed to be enjoying the intrigue of it all. "I could have sworn, at least twice, I heard Saul tell her 'don't worry, Bunny, there's no way he knows.'"

I straightened. "There's no way he knows?" I asked to make sure.

Dana nodded once. "Yes, that's what I heard him say. It occurred to me then that his friend Bunny might have a husband or boyfriend."

I startled when the nail gun started back up. Dana laughed. "Don't worry. I was jumping every time that machine started up, but now I'm used to it. You will be too if you have some remodeling done. Is it for Evie's cottage?"

"No, I bought a rundown building. I'm hoping to turn it into a new bakery."

Dana perked up. "A new bakery in Ripple Creek? Oh, I hope you start it soon. Will you carry fresh bread?" She closed her eyes and took a big whiff as if she smelled fresh bread right there in her living room. "I love fresh bread with jam or butter. I could live on it. I don't need anything else, just fresh bread."

"Once you have your new kitchen, you'll be ready to bake all kinds of delicious food," I reminded her.

"Yes, but I've never learned how to make bread properly."

I placed my hand on hers. "Then you're in luck because I'm planning to bake fresh bread."

"Wonderful! I'm so happy you dropped by." She walked me to the door.

I paused before stepping out of the clamor and the air filled with sawdust. "Dana, just for the sake of it—do you hunt?"

Her eyes rounded. "Heavens no. Guns scare me witless. I prefer to see the deer walking around with their bodies attached."

I laughed. "I couldn't agree more. Thanks for chatting with me."

"Tell Evie I say hello," she called as I headed back to my car.

That was one suspect to cross off the list. Now, it was time to talk to Saul's brother-in-law.

thirty-one

. . .

M ilner Realty was housed in an early twentieth century bungalow just a few miles below the Miramont resort. There was a welcoming set of wicker chairs on the front porch. Photos of real estate listings hung in the front windows. They blocked an incredible view of the river as it meandered over rocks and around secret, shady nooks on its way to Ripple Creek.

A sign with the word welcome stretched out between two elks hung on the front door. I knocked lightly as I opened the door.

"Yes, come in. We're open," a voice called from within. I recognized it as Kent's voice. Was I getting closer to Saul's killer, and, if so—why was I getting closer to a killer? My first unofficial case nearly ended in calamity once I'd finally pinpointed the right suspect. I certainly didn't want a repeat of that. But if I wanted to move forward with my investigation, I was going to have to take some bold steps. With that in mind, I took a deep breath and proceeded into the real estate office.

Outside, it was a charming bungalow with rich historic details like dormers, a stone front porch and a stained glass transom over the front door. It had an awesome location too. Real estate agents always managed to snag the best properties for themselves. The interior still had some of that nostalgic charisma as well. The wide door trim and moulding was a rich, reddish oak, and built-in shelves surrounded a small room that looked out over the river. Back when it was still a home, the space was probably used as the owner's study. Now it housed a desk, a file cabinet and a copy machine.

Kent came out of a back room, his office, presumably. He didn't recognize me at first. "I'm Kent Milner." His long, bushy sideburns fit the era of the house we were standing in. He stuck out his hand.

"Scottie Ramone. We met at my bakery cart during the farmer's market."

"Yes, of course. Wonderful cinnamon rolls, by the way. How can I help you?" He didn't strike me as a person who'd just lost a family member.

"I was on my way up to see a friend at the resort, and I saw your sign so I thought I'd stop in and see how you were doing. I heard about your brother-in-law, Saul."

His face drooped more into the soft jowls that were

hanging off his jaw. "It's been such a shock. I still can't believe it. My wife is beside herself with grief. Saul was her only sibling. Saul and I didn't always get along, but Margaret loved her brother. They had a tough upbringing, moved from place to place with a father who was about as loving and supportive as a pine cone. Saul was all Margaret had back then."

It was an entirely different narrative than the first time Kent spoke about his brother-in-law. I needed to bring it up, or this whole visit was a waste of time.

"That's nice to hear, but the last time we spoke—you advised me to warn my friend, Cade Rafferty, off hiring Saul to work around the Gramby Estate."

Again, his expression drooped. "Yes, and I feel just terrible about that. My last conversation with Saul was angry and terse. He owed me some money. I feel awful that I kept pushing him for it. It was only a few hundred dollars. It was the principal of the thing," he said sharply as if he was talking to his wife. He shook his head. "I should have let it go. Now he's gone, and I can't ever apologize about the way I spoke to him."

"This might sound strange, but I was at the Gramby Estate the day Saul was shot. I was looking around, and I found a crumpled, handwritten note. It was asking for the money or else."

Kent's expression hardened a smidgen, but I wasn't getting killer vibes from him. "I didn't realize you were part of the investigation. Ranger Braddock said he was moving forward with the notion that Mr. Rafferty was the intended target, and Saul was in the wrong place at the wrong time."

"I'm not part of the investigation," I corrected. "I just felt a connection to the whole thing because Mr. Rafferty is my friend, and I happened to show up at the same time as the emergency crews. I heard word that the official investigation was looking into the possibility that Mr. Rafferty was the target. That puts my friend in danger. I suppose I'm just trying to find out what happened that day, and since little evidence was left behind, at least according to Mr. Rafferty, I was, as they say, looking under every rock to see if I could help. I happened to find the note because it was on the ground near Saul's van." My longwinded explanation seemed to do the trick.

Kent's stance relaxed again. "That note was also unfortunate. I was frustrated with Saul. He was taking advantage of me just like he took advantage of his customers. I suppose that's why I kept on him about the few hundred dollars. He needed some consequences." His eyes widened. "Not that I think murder is the appropriate consequence to anything."

"No, of course not."

I wasn't getting any sense that the man standing in front of me had shot his brother-in-law in cold blood. There were no mounted animal heads on the walls, which wasn't surprising in a realtor's office, but I wasn't seeing anything that indicated Kent was a hunter. That was just an assumption based on the interior of his business and the fact that I just couldn't picture the man with the ill-fitting suit and brightly colored tie wearing camouflage and hiding out in a duck blind. That was probably my one piece of evidence that meant anything in the case. The killer had to have excellent aim and had to know how to handle a rifle. I was sure only a small percent of the population had both attributes.

"Kent, can you tell me—was Saul having trouble with anyone else? Was he dating someone, someone who, I don't know, let's say might have been married or attached?"

I startled when something soft tickled the back of my leg. I glanced down. A gray striped cat with an extremely fluffy tail rubbed himself against my calf.

"Boston, where did you come from?" Kent said to the cat. The cat heard his name, stopped its trip around my legs and sat down with a confident meow. Kent looked at his watch. "I guess he's letting me know it's time for his lunch."

I leaned down to pet the cat. He pushed against my hand and purred.

"You were asking about Saul's social life," Kent said. I was thrilled he'd picked the conversation back up. "He was constantly seeing different women. I've been married to his sister for twenty years. In all that time, I don't think he ever considered proposing or settling down. Regardless of his middle-aged hairline and paunch, the ladies still seemed to come around."

"Did he ever get himself into trouble with an angry husband or boyfriend?" I was probably grasping at straws now, but my first two leads had gone astray. It seemed I was no closer to figuring this whole mess out.

Kent rubbed his chin. "You know, I think there have been a few of those situations. They're the kind of thing Margaret keeps mostly to herself. She never liked to talk badly about her brother. But I do remember a husband making threats against Saul, showing up at his apartment and making such a ruckus the police were called."

I perked up. "When did this happen? What was the husband's name?"

"Heck if I know. It happened a good ten years ago."

I un-perked. "Was he seeing anyone recently?"

Boston had moved his ankle parade over to Kent's pant legs. He was not going to give up until lunch was served.

Kent shook his head. "Margaret might have mentioned something about it, but I tended to tune out when she was talking about Saul's social life. It changed more than the weather up on the peaks."

Boston let out a loud, scowling meow.

Kent laughed. "I better feed him before he starts yowling."

"Thanks for talking to me."

"Remember, if you have any realty needs, Kent is your man." You had to love a salesperson. No matter what happened in their lives, there was still a sales pitch to deliver.

I walked outside. The sun was at midday intensity. I was no closer to finding out who had killed Saul Bonelli. Was I wasting time? Was Cade actually the target?

I growled in frustration. This one was a mind boggler.

I did a quick mental inventory of what I knew about the case. Focus on Saul's social life had settled firmly in my head. I knew one thing for certain. Someone named Bunny had left a sweet note and cookies in Saul's lunch pail. And those cookies were wrapped in a napkin from Castillo's Deli. The deli was about five miles farther up the hill. I was already halfway there. It was probably just another goose in my wild goose chase, but I didn't have anything to lose.

thirty-two

. . .

I might have been to Castillo's Deli three or four times in
the past twenty years. They had delicious ravioli. I
decided since I was up the mountain it would be a nice
surprise to bring Nana some ravioli for dinner. The original
owner, Frank Castillo, died while I was away studying
pastries in Paris. I vaguely recollected Nana mentioning that
Frank left the deli to his son, Damian or Dominic or something like that.

The shop was located on a corner right below the Miramont Resort. Most of the shops along the same block were
exclusive clothing and art boutiques. The deli had held its
own even as the whole town morphed into a playground for
the wealthy. Castillo's Deli had a rustic brick exterior. Large
salamis wrapped in wax and tied up with rough twine hung
in the front windows next to sprigs of dried thyme and
oregano. The smell of garlic was enough to make my eyes

water as I stepped into the crowded shop. I grabbed a number and found an empty niche behind the rotating stand of chips and cookies. One could have imagined they'd just stepped into a bustling deli in New York the way the sales clerks were yelling out numbers and orders. Two young men, both in white aprons, stood behind a glass shield, piling long rolls with pungent cheeses and sandwich meats.

Everyone was bustling around as if their hair was on fire. As I scanned the workers behind the counter, I couldn't find anyone who looked old enough to be the son of Frank Castillo. There was, however, one middle-aged woman standing at the hot food section shoveling large chunks of lasagna into a foil tray. She didn't look terribly happy. In fact, if I were to make a judgment call, I'd say she looked down-right distressed. As I waited for my turn at the counter, I noticed the same woman, more than once, pull a tissue out of her pocket to blot her eyes. The other counter workers were young. If I'd ever seen Frank Castillo's son, I had no recollection of what he looked like. I was sure he had to be in his fifties or sixties.

The activity was finally slowing down. I must have arrived right at the prime lunch hour. I was only two numbers away. The women in front of me were mostly interested in the Italian pastries in the sweets section. I was planning to ask the woman with the tissue and occasional tears if she knew someone named Bunny when luck smiled down on me. A fifty-something man with a barrel chest, a curled up moustache and a booming voice popped out from the kitchen area. A white apron seemed to be held on by the fold of his big belly. It was covered with tomato sauce and grease. "Bunny, how are we doing on the lasagna?" he bellowed. There weren't enough people left in the store for that level of voice, but he seemed agitated about something. Although, if I really thought about it, a bellow was always deemed appropriate in the middle of a deli. I'd been to some popular delis in New York where the casual chatting was at such a decibel it was almost impossible to hear the person behind the counter.

The woman, Bunny, leaned into the hot tray area. "We could use another tray, Damian," she said weakly. Her frail, unsteady tone was a sharp contrast to the man who I now had pegged as the owner of the deli.

My luck continued when Bunny, my reason for the visit, called my number. I walked up to the counter. She did her best to produce a smile. Bunny was fifty-something, petite, with honey yellow streaked hair that was parted on the side. Her lips were heavily covered with pink lipstick, and each cheek had a rosy dot of rouge. "What can I get you?"

"I'll take two pounds of your ricotta and mushroom ravioli to go, please." I was glad I'd come up with the ravioli idea. It gave me an opening with Bunny. At the same time, it would be a nice surprise for Nana.

Bunny set to work filling a foil container with ravioli. The aromas in the deli were making me hungry. I was looking forward to dinner. I needed to ignore my growling stomach and pop into action. "I'm taking my friend dinner. He had a terrible thing happen." I talked over the countertop and was glad that the earlier clamor had calmed. "He had a handyman working at his house, and the man from Saul Fixes All was shot dead." As I said the name Saul, she dropped three raviolis on the counter. That flustered her more, and she nearly dropped the foil container. She placed it hastily on the counter. "I'm sorry, I'm very clumsy today," she muttered and looked around for a cloth to wipe away the spilled food.

I was risking not getting any ravioli, but the case was my priority. I decided to take the next step. I lowered my voice more. "You're Bunny. You're the one who left the cookies in Saul's lunch box."

She looked slowly up from the marinara mess she'd made with big eyes. "How did you know about the cookies?" She glanced quickly behind her toward the kitchen. "Wait a moment. We can talk outside?" She finished filling the container. I added a loaf of Italian bread to the order because what was ravioli without bread.

"Cherise," Bunny said to one of the girls. "I'm taking a break." She took off her apron and walked out from behind the counter. I carried my purchase out behind her.

Bunny kept walking, presumably, to be out of view from inside the deli. We stopped in front of the ski apparel shop. "How did you know about the cookies?"

"I arrived at my friend's house just as the emergency crews were assessing the situation."

Bunny's face lost color. Even her rouge seemed to fade. "Did you see him? Did you see Saul?" She sobbed once and took out her tissue.

"I did. If it's any comfort, I think he died instantly. He didn't know it was coming."

She sobbed into her tissue and nodded. "That's good to hear. Did you know Saul?" For a second, she surveyed me head to toe as if she was wondering whether I was a rival for his affections.

"I didn't know him, but his van was parked at my friend's house. I figured the police would need to find next of kin, so I looked around in his van for something that would give us names or phone numbers. I found his lunch pail. In my search, I decided to open it. That was when I found the cookies with your note on a deli napkin."

It seemed to be dawning on her that I hadn't just decided to drive up the hill for ravioli.

"You came to the deli to find me. Why?" she asked.

I sighed. "I'll come clean. The police seem to think the killer accidentally shot Saul instead of my friend. I'm trying to find out the truth. Was Saul your boyfriend?" I hadn't asked it particularly loud, but she winced as if I'd yelled it out for the world to hear.

"Shh, I don't want my husband to hear."

"Husband? Oh, I see. So, you're married to—" I let her fill in the blank.

"Damian Castillo is my husband." She said it as if the phrase left a bitter taste in her mouth. She covered her face with both hands and shook her head. When she pulled her hands away there were white fingerprints on her forehead. "What have I done? This is my fault."

"How is it your fault?"

She glanced back toward the deli. The strong scent of garlic wafted toward us as a customer stepped inside. Bunny turned back to me. "I think Damian knew. You see, our marriage—well, I considered it over long ago. Damian had an affair with one of our counter clerks. It went on right under my nose for three years until I caught them in the storage closet." A shade of red passed over her complexion. "He told me he'd stopped the affair. I fired the woman. For a short while I thought maybe I could get past his indiscretion."

I hardly would have termed a three-year affair, almost in plain view, an indiscretion but, I assumed that was the easiest way for Bunny to accept it. "How long were you with Saul?" Just saying his name made her eyes glitter with more tears.

"Saul used to come into the deli every Tuesday for our sandwich special. Tuesday is meatball sandwich day. He was always so charming and treated me like I existed, do you know what I mean? He saw me. He looked right into my eyes and listened with his whole heart whenever I spoke. Damian wouldn't look my direction if my hair was on fire. Only, I think—" she stopped short. "I should get back inside."

"You think what?" I asked, a little too anxiously.

"I think Damian started realizing something was up between us. All of a sudden he was bringing me flowers and paying me little compliments. 'Bunny, your eyes are sparkling today.' 'Bunny, what's that incredible perfume you're wearing?'" She chuckled. "Trust me, if you stand all day in a deli, the only perfume you're wearing is garlic and oregano."

"Was Damian jealous?" I was getting right to the heart of a motive before she went back inside.

"It was probably just my imagination. Although, last week, when Saul came into the deli for his sandwich, Damian came out of the kitchen to wait on him. He sent me to the storeroom for cans of tomatoes. That's a task he always does himself, and Damian doesn't work the counter unless some of our staff call in sick. We were fully staffed that day. And he wasn't very friendly to Saul either. He slapped three meatballs on a roll. We always put five on our sandwiches. He practically threw the sandwich at Saul."

"Bunny"—Cherise popped her head out of the shop door—"I need more change from the safe."

"Be right there." Bunny turned to me. "I've got to get back to work. Thank you for stopping by. I know we don't know each other, but it has made me feel better being able to talk to someone about all this. I couldn't very well talk to my family." With that, she nodded and hurried back to the deli.

I carried my ravioli and bread to the car and climbed inside. A quick Google search gave me the address of Damian Castillo. If Bunny and Damian were at work, it stood to reason that their house was empty. Maybe I could do a casual glance around the property. With any luck, I'd stumble upon a dirt bike. I had no idea if I was any closer to finding out who killed Saul Bonelli, but one thing was sure—Damian Castillo had motive. Was it enough to push him to murder?

thirty-three

. . .

Most of the neighborhoods around the Miramont
Resort were upper middle class and high-end. The
Castillo residence, a mid-century modern with a great deal of
glass was in a nice neighborhood where the homes had paved
driveways and oversized garages for things like snowmobiles
and ski equipment. The Castillo's garage was at the top of a
somewhat steep driveway. Interestingly enough, the garage
door was open. I considered for a moment that the open
garage door meant someone was at home, but there were no
cars in the driveway or, for that matter, in the garage.

My heart was beating fast at the notion that I was walking
up someone's private driveway without being invited. If
someone was home, I planned to use the excuse that I was
looking for a friend's house, and I'd seemingly gotten the
wrong directions.

As I reached the top of the driveway, it was more apparent

than ever that no one was at home. It was easy enough to accidentally drive away leaving the garage door open. Perhaps, Damian Castillo had been too preoccupied after murdering his wife's lover to think about hitting the garage remote.

The garage was a luxury space complete with poured stone floor and built-in oak shelves. A shiny silver refrigerator sat in one corner, and boxes marked Christmas and Halloween decorations were piled in the opposite corner. I made quick and significant discoveries. The first didn't help me much with the case. There was no dirt bike in the garage. If Damian did like to putter around on the trails in his spare time, he was storing the bike elsewhere. The second discovery was a stunner, and even though I'd come to the property hoping to spot the dirt bike, this new revelation was much more significant. Unless sweet, little Bunny liked to shoot animals, I could only conclude that Damian Castillo was an avid hunter. Glass deer and elk eyes stared at me from every wall in the garage. Each head professionally mounted on polished mahogany. Either Bunny had given a hard no about hanging dead animal *trophies* in her lovely home, or Damian had killed so many of them, he'd run out of wall space and had to hang the overflow in his garage.

I glanced around. The pairs of glass eyes were admittedly giving me the creeps. They all seemed to be saying 'you're trespassing', which I was. I'd found what I considered to be a big piece of evidence. It was easy to conclude that the person who shot Saul from a good distance had skilled aim—like an experienced hunter. I snapped a few photos of the garage. I would only show Cade because I was sure it would interest him. However, since I was breaking the law, I'd leave Dalton out of the loop. I was just about to make a hasty retreat when the rattling sound of a dirt bike came buzzing up the driveway.

My heart skipped back to overdrive. Suddenly, my excuse of looking for a friend's house seemed flimsy and lame. I looked around and dashed toward the stacked boxes of holiday decorations. Thankfully, the Castillos liked to trim their house in the holiday spirit. The boxes were stacked high and wide enough for me to hide behind them.

The motor of the bike echoed in the garage, shaking some of the antlers on the wall. It turned off abruptly. I peered around one of the boxes. The rider was pulling off a motor-cycle helmet. It was a young man, eighteen to twenty years old. The dust on his face surrounding the clean spots left behind by the goggles indicated that he'd been out on the trails for a long ride. I could only assume that the young man was Castillo's son. He pushed his helmet onto one of the shelves and strutted out the way only a young man could pull off. I breathed a sigh of relief thinking I was going to be able to skedaddle unnoticed. Then the roar of a garage door rumbled overhead and the heavy door slid majestically down as the kid walked out of the garage.

I waited a few minutes to listen for his footsteps getting farther from the garage. I climbed out from my hiding spot. The automatic light turned off as soon as the large door reached its final destination. The dirt bike was still giving off the warm, pungent smell of gasoline as it cooled down from its workout. It was so quiet I could hear the walls crackle with the heat of the midday sun. The refrigerator made a gurgling sound that turned into a low hum. All of a sudden, I was standing in a mostly dark garage with the dead stares of many mounted animal heads glaring at me from each wall.

"It wasn't me," I told them holding my hands up in surrender. I'd never shot anything more dangerous than a water pistol. I was certain I'd given the young man more than enough time to get inside the house. It was a warm enough day that I was sure an expensive house like that had its central air conditioning running at full tilt. He wouldn't hear the garage door slide open and shut. I planned to only open it enough to duck down, slip out and hightail it down the steep driveway. (Maybe not hightail because of the steep slope but at least a quick trot).

I reached for the metal handle on the inside of the door and gave it a good yank. It didn't budge. In fact, it stood so solidly shut, I hurt my shoulder. I rubbed it, took a deep breath and tried again. No movement at all. I glanced around the walls for a button or some kind of an emergency release, but the only things I found were light switches and a switch that shut off the refrigerator. I turned it back on. I worried that Damian or Bunny or someone in the household had a phone app that would let them know when lights or appliances were being turned on or off, so I ended my quest for a door release. It seemed I'd gotten myself stuck in the Castillo's garage. At least there was food and drink if I was trapped for a long time. That reminded me of the raviolis that were now heating up in my warm car. Much longer and they wouldn't be safe to eat.

One wall had a heavy gray blind covering a window. I hurried over. The blind, too, seemed to be mechanical. What-ever happened to people opening their own garage doors and blinds? I figured out how to slide the blind open with a switch at the top. The window looked out on the side of the property opposite the house. That was convenient. Now, I just need to slide it open, jump out and take off. I was literally the world's worst trespasser because I quickly realized that the window was locked and about as easy to open as the mechanical garage door.

A few levers later, I heard the window click open. I slid it as much as I needed to hoist myself up and out of the garage. I breathed a huge sigh of relief as my feet landed in the pine needle debris outside the building. Closing the window from the outside was harder than opening it from the inside. I fussed with it for a few seconds, but the whole attempt was cut short when something hard poked me from behind.

I froze and put my hands up, an instinctual response to a gun being jammed into my back.

"Hold it right there." The voice was young and raspy, and while I hadn't heard him talk, I knew without looking back that Damian Castillo's son was standing behind me with a gun.

thirty-four

. . .

"**W**ell, lady, why don't you start talking? What are you stealing from our garage?"

I held up both hands and turned slowly around. He looked even younger close up, but he seemed pretty darn confident with the long rifle in his hands.

It was me and the angry looking kid with the gun. With the way he held it, I assumed he knew how to handle it. I tried to assure myself that at least it wouldn't go off accidentally.

"I wasn't trying to steal anything," I said, shocked at how confident my tone was considering my insides had turned to jelly. I decided to pivot back to my original plan. "I was looking for my friend's house. I can see I turned up at the wrong place because she doesn't have a son. I walked into the garage because it was open. I was drawn to all the hunting trophies. My father used to hunt, and he'd take me with him, occasionally. It was great fun, out under the stars, sitting by the campfire eating s'mores."

He laughed dryly. "That sounds like a girl scout campout not a hunting trip." He was astute. Since I'd never been even close to attending a hunting trip and since my father had been more of a jetsetter in cashmere suit type than a roughing it guy in camouflage we obviously never went on a hunting trip.

I shrugged. "What can I say? My dad liked s'mores. Did you kill all those animals?" I looked pointedly at the very long, very deadly gun.

A slight grin formed through the angry scowl. "I shot a few of them. One day, I'll be as good a shot as my dad."

"Your dad? You're learning those hunting skills from him?" I'd landed on a topic that interested him. He seemed to temporarily forget that he was holding me prisoner with a weapon.

"My dad was a sniper in the army. He could shoot a target from 1200 meters. I'm going to join the army next year and learn how to be a sniper, just like my dad."

"Sounds like you're proud of your dad. Good for you." What I didn't add was the tiny inconvenience that his highly trained dad might also be a murderer. I didn't have any evidence except there was motive, and the killer was skilled at shooting targets from a long distance. I had no doubt there were plenty of hunters on the mountainside, but how many were army snipers? And how many had found out that their wife was having an affair with the victim. I was no expert, but all arrows were pointing to Damian Castillo as the killer.

"Yeah, I'm proud of him. What's wrong with that?" It was said in a sort of rebellious teen tone, the tone we all used at that young age when we went on defense even when someone suggested something nice.

"Nothing wrong with that at all." I glanced side to side wondering if there was a way for me to slip off, but since I didn't have the superpower talents needed to outrun a bullet, I had to stay put.

"You'll meet him in a second. Then you can explain to him why you were climbing out the garage window." His angry scowl returned, and he was wearing a smirk of pride as if he'd just caught a stealthy prey.

"You—your dad is coming here?" I asked after the weight of his words finally took hold.

"That's right. When my phone app told me the garage window was being opened, I called to let him know we had a burglar. He said he was heading straight home."

Those darn phone apps. I should have known a nice house with a Fort Knox style garage door would have a lot of security features. What on earth was I going to tell his dad? I could always just tell him the truth, but I was fairly certain I would be the next head mounted in the garage.

"You don't need him to come. I told you, I was lost and wandered into the open garage to admire the hunting trophies."

"Yeah, you said that."

An idea popped into my head. Did a household with a lot of security features in place ever leave without closing the garage? "Well, if he comes, then he'll know that you left the garage door open. I'll bet he won't be happy about that." I'd gotten to him. His angry, stalwart posture loosened. Then he looked highly suspicious. Not the response I was hoping for.

"Wait a minute—" he said. He kept the gun barrel pointed on me like a laser. "I didn't see you when I rode up just now. You were hiding. So you *were* there to steal from us."

"I hid because I got scared. I heard your loud motorcycle, and I realized I shouldn't have been standing in your garage. I ducked behind some boxes and waited for you to leave. I planned to walk away then, but you shut the door and I couldn't get it open." Was I digging myself in deeper? Probably. In my defense, my mind was too preoccupied with what I was going to say to Damian Castillo. I chuckled lightly, nervously. "What could I have possibly stolen? I don't think I could carry off that refrigerator, and I've already got far too many holiday decorations piled up in my own garage."

"You said it yourself, you walked in to admire the hunting trophies. It costs a lot of money to have a head mounted properly. Maybe you decided you'd walk out with one or two."

I'd already lied about my nostalgic, non-existent hunting trips, so I couldn't very well tell him that I preferred to see the deer out in nature than on a wall. It seemed I'd run into an even more stubborn version of myself at eighteen.

"Look, if I was stealing something—" I held out my arms wider. "Wouldn't I have it on me? I'm empty handed. Just like when I stepped into your garage."

He squinted one eye at me. "What's the name of the friend?" he asked.

"Friend?" I'd gotten so tangled up in my fibs, I'd forgotten my original one. "Oh right, my friend. The one I came to visit. Uh, her name is—my gaze flicked around. Why on earth was it so hard to make up a name when there were literally millions of possibilities? "Her name is Bonnie, Bonnie Spruce." (Yes, the surname came from the blue spruce towering over the driveway.)

"That's a lie. I know everyone around here, and no one named Bonnie Spruce lives in the neighborhood."

"Maybe I got the last name wrong," I suggested.

He shook his head. "There's no one named Bonnie either."

I had to run into the one teenager who actually knew the names of his neighbors. "Look, I'll walk away. Nothing's been taken, and I'm sure you have things to look at on your phone." I hoped that suggestion would remind him that he'd let a significant amount of time go by since he last looked at his phone. But, no, it seemed I'd also found the one teenager in a thousand mile radius who wasn't inextricably glued to his phone.

"Good try, lady."

I never minded being called a lady, but it was all about context and this was not the right context.

"You're going to pull your dad away from his busy deli to come all the way home—" I realized my big snafu several seconds after I said it, especially when his expression flashed back to convey major suspicion.

"How do you know my dad owns a deli? I thought you were lost and looking for *Bonnie Spruce*," he said the name with extra derision.

"I am up here looking for Bonnie. Maybe you don't know everyone like you think you do. Maybe you don't know Bonnie." I added in a chin lift. "And I figured this was Damian Castillo's house because you look just like your father."

He grinned. "I was adopted."

"Oh, well, the resemblance is remarkable. Quite the coincidence." I forced up a sheepish grin. It seemed I had many talents, mostly with yeast dough and sugary batters, but I was a first-rate terrible liar. That might have been Nana's fault. She always knew when I was fibbing or embellishing. My forays into the world of little white lies had to get bolder and more outlandish. It didn't matter. She always knew. She claimed my eyes blinked a lot whenever I was lying. I tried the test in the mirror several times, but I never saw it. I supposed that was just another one of Nana's superpowers. I sure could have used my superhero.

"Like I said, you can explain why you're here to my dad. He just pulled around the corner. I guess it's time to start coming up with your next lie."

I smirked at him. "Like you haven't lied yourself." A lifted truck, a hunter's truck, rumbled gently as it pulled up to the top of the driveway. Damian Castillo was sitting behind the steering wheel. He did not look pleased. Oh, Scottie, what have you gotten yourself into this time?

thirty-five

. . .

N ow that he wasn't wearing a marinara stained apron, Damian Castillo looked far more menacing as he tromped toward us in work boots. As he approached I temporarily forgot my terrible predicament and asked myself whether or not the man walking toward me was a killer. Yes, yes he was. I would have bet my almond croissant recipe on it. Goodie, I'd solved the murder. At the same time, it seemed I might become a casualty. I panicked, my heart beating faster with each plodding step of his large boots.

"Your son left the garage door open. I came up the driveway hoping to find someone, so I could let you know your garage was open." It flowed out smoothly and in the exact way my fifteen-year-old self would have said it.

His son wasn't impressed. "Was that seriously all you could come up with?"

I shrugged. "I thought it sounded good."

Damian reached us. He put his fists on his hips and stared at me with flared nostrils. "Tony said you were climbing out of the garage. What were you trying to steal?"

I sighed. "Look, I wasn't stealing anything. I mean, do I look like a thief?"

Damian's curlicue moustache rocked back and forth. "Thieves come in all shapes and sizes." He squinted at me. "Didn't I just see you in the deli? You walked outside with Bunny."

"See, I knew this lady was up to something," Tony boasted.

His dad seemed to be putting a few pieces together. They were not pieces that worked in my favor. He reached for the gun. In an act of defiance, Tony held onto it just a second longer than he should have. I was his prey, and he was not pleased about having to hand me over.

"Go inside, son. I need to talk to the thief alone." Tony walked away even more reluctantly than he handed over the rifle.

The gun poked me again and I gasped. "Now talk. Why were you talking to Bunny? Why were you snooping around my garage?"

"I understand you're quite the hunter," I started. I had no idea where I was heading with it, but my heartbeat was drowning out any rational thoughts. "Tony tells me you were a sniper in the army. He's very proud of you."

"The kid has a big mouth." Normally, a curly moustache would give a man a dapper, old-fashioned look. Not the case with Damian. He was mean through and through, and if he was a sniper in the army there was a good chance he'd already killed someone. Murdering Saul probably hadn't taken much thought. "Start talking before I call the police."

"The police. You're right. That's who should handle this situation. Obviously, I've been trespassing and—"

"Never mind the police. Why were you talking to Bunny? What did she tell you?"

I tried to weigh my options only to realize there were none. Even if I managed to somehow knock the big guy off his feet, it wouldn't take him much time to recover and get control of the gun. With his skills, he could shoot me even if I raced through the forest or down the highway. He was certainly a treacherous opponent. "I was asking Bunny if she knew a friend of mine."

"What friend?"

I straightened my posture. "Saul Bonelli." He flinched, as expected.

"What about him?" he asked darkly, pushing the gun against my stomach. I'd never had a gun pointed at me. If I survived this ordeal, I hoped to never have the experience again.

Right then, my phone rang, startling me. My reflexes automatically told me to answer it. I pulled it out of my pocket. Adrenaline raced through me when the name Dalton came up on the screen. I answered it fast. "Dalton, I'm at Damian Castillo's—" It was all I got out before Damian smacked the phone painfully from my hand. The phone flew onto the driveway and bounced several times before stopping against the tire on the truck.

"Let's go," Damian said.

"Where are we going?" I asked, my voice shaky. This whole thing had taken an even more dangerous turn. Why had I gotten involved in this in the first place? I should have left it to Dalton. I was blaming him and his flippant attitude toward me. I wanted to show him, and now, he was going to have to solve my murder as well.

I felt like I was being walked to the gallows as Damian poked my back with the tip of the gun. We passed his garage and a nicely paved covered patio. There was a section of lawn set up with a putting green. Beyond that it was all wilderness. He was looking for a place to kill me, a place where only the squirrels and deer could be witness to my tragic demise.

I walked clumsily along, not able to concentrate on my steps or the pathway ahead of me. We were heading toward the spot where Damian would kill me. For a stretch of time, perhaps from self-preservation to keep myself from freaking out, I slipped into a sort of out-of-body experience. I was definitely there, gun in my back and the vast wilderness ahead of me, but part of my brain was watching the whole thing from above. The two of us were getting deeper into the forest. Soon we'd be out of earshot or at least far enough that no one would question the sound of the shot and its reverberation through the trees. After all, there were always plenty of hunters up in these mountains. If only we'd happened upon one right then.

My options were still limited. I could make a run for it, maybe zigzagging or ducking to avoid the bullet. If I did nothing, I would surely be heading toward my execution. The word sent a chill through me. My mind and body came back together into one terrified human.

I stepped on the biggest stone on the path. It wobbled side to side, nearly pitching me to the ground. In that instant, an idea popped into my head. I spun around exactly when Damian stepped onto the same stone. It wobbled. The gun barrel swung to the side as he tried to keep from falling over. I gave him a little help... in the opposite direction. I shoved my hands against him. What had started as an unsteady step due to the wobbly rock turned into a lumbering fall backward. The gun swung back and forth as he tried to steady himself, but the inertia had begun and he was no small man. He stumbled back more, tripped over a tree root. I didn't stick around for the rest. I knew enough about high school physics to know the big guy was going down. I heard the grunt and thud behind me as I took off at a NASCAR pace toward the trees.

A shot rang out. I ducked behind a wide trunk. Damian's footsteps shook the ground like an earthquake as he barreled toward me, angrier than ever. I searched frantically around and found a three-foot tree limb that had snapped off in the wind. It wasn't as thick and heavy as I would have liked, but I was sure it could cause some pain. As his footsteps neared, I grasped the end of the branch in both hands and lifted it back like a baseball bat. If only I had an actual baseball bat at that moment.

The barrel of his long rifle made its appearance before the hunter. I swung the branch as hard as I could and smacked him across the face. The gun went off from the impact. It startled me so much, I didn't take off in time. Damian regained his bearings faster. Blood trickled down his cheek. He wiped at it and growled at me. "You're going to die."

"I don't think that's how this ends," a deep voice said from behind the tree. "Place the rifle on the ground, put your hands on your neck and turn around slowly." The voice was so familiar and I was so thrilled to hear it, I hopped out from behind the trunk. Dalton didn't look the least bit surprised to see me.

"You all right?" he asked while keeping his unflinching focus on Damian.

"I'm fine. I guess you know then that Mr. Castillo killed Saul." I could speak freely now about my conclusions, and it felt great.

"I do. Now, head back down, Scottie. I need to make an arrest."

I wanted badly to hang out and watch the whole arrest drama unfold, but I had the ravioli to consider. They'd spent far too long in the hot car as it was.

thirty-six

· · ·

Nana and I sat on her front stoop, and I relayed to her the entire story. Saying it aloud made me shiver a few times. I'd had a gun pressed against me for a long period of time. It was amazing I didn't break down into hysterics. Nana insisted it was the adrenaline. It helped all of us keep our heads at times when we most needed them. I was sure hysterics would have made one of the angry Castillo men pull the trigger.

Nana put her arm around my shoulder after I'd concluded the whole harrowing tale. "Next time, I'll just make homemade ravioli." We had a good laugh, but deep down, the horror of what could have happened had us both quaking.

Tires grinding over gravel pulled our attention to the corner. Dalton's truck turned onto Rainbow Road.

"That's my cue to leave." Nana braced her hand on my shoulder and stood up. That was a new thing. Normally, she could lift herself from the step without much effort. Being active and always positively grounded had kept her as spry as a twenty-year-old. I never liked to let the thought take hold, but I knew someday Nana would slow down. But not today. She practically trotted up the steps in her hurry to leave me alone on the front porch.

I glanced back at her before she slipped inside. "I'll bet you a million dollars that he's *not* here to propose."

She stopped in the doorway. "That would be a silly bet considering only one of us could deliver on it. But I will bake you a batch of oatmeal cookies if he showed up with a ring." She closed the door at the same time that Dalton was opening his.

I knew, too well, it wasn't going to be a proposal, just a lecture about stepping into business I had no business stepping into.

I stood up and dusted off my bottom. Sitting on a step with a dusty bottom was not going to give me the confidence I needed to face my scolding.

"Before you start telling me how stupid it was for me to go up to Castillo's place, I just want to mention that I had no idea he was the killer until, well, the whole hunting me through the forest like prey part of the day."

His face blanched a little as I said it. "You're right. I should be standing here chewing you out. In fact, I should be hand-cuffing and arresting you for obstructing an investigation."

"What obstruction? There was no obstruction. In fact, I beat you to the punch."

He took off his dark sunglasses. It erased some of that official police look. (Although, that worked on him too.) He pushed the glasses into his pocket. "You did. But that was only because you were in the area. I was still in town when I figured out this whole mess."

I crossed my arms and tilted my head at him. "Exactly how did you figure it out? Forensics? Ballistics? You know, the easy way?"

"Now you're just being cocky."

"I am but it's not every day a woman corners a murderer."

He cleared his throat. "I think the murderer had you cornered. That was until the tall, handsome policeman stepped in to save the day."

I shrugged. "I suppose you're fairly tall."

His right cheek dimpled. "I guess I don't need to tell you that was a dangerous thing to do."

"Considering I was the one standing at the opposite end of a hunting rifle, I'm well aware. You still haven't told me how you found out it was Damian."

"Well, Saul's sister mentioned she thought he was having an affair with Bunny Castillo, and I happened to know that Damian was an army sniper. I was heading to the deli to question him. First, I phoned my friend Scottie and got the strangest answer."

"I tried to give you more details, but he knocked the phone out of my hand."

"My heart was beating so wildly the whole drive up to the house I thought my ribs might break."

I smiled. "Can that really happen?"

"Probably not. But that brings me to the reason for my visit."

I lifted my chin. "Go ahead. Fire away. I can take it."

"I'm glad you're all right, Scottie." Without warning he took hold of my hand and pulled me in for a long hug. Talk about melting like butter on a hot sidewalk...

Scottie Ramone Cozy Mystery Book 2

about the author

London Lovett is author of the Port Danby, Starfire, Firefly Junction, Scottie Ramone and Frostfall Island Cozy Mystery series. She loves getting caught up in a good mystery and baking delicious, new treats!

Learn more at:
www.londonlovett.com

Printed in Great Britain
by Amazon